"You're hurting me."

He raised his brow. "Am I? Then maybe you'll tell me what you know about Mr. Tuttle."

"I don't know anything."

He twisted Becca's arm behind her back. His free hand closed around her throat. "Let's go over this again. You were going to tell me where Mr. Tuttle kept his papers. Or maybe he mentioned computer files or an external hard drive."

"The Amish do not have computers, so I do not know what you are talking about."

He leaned close to her ear. "What *do* you know about? He had to have told you something."

She remained silent.

"Come on, lady. Talk."

But she couldn't talk because his hand was tight on her neck. She tried to scream. The effort took more air than she could muster. Her head spun, and her lungs burned. Her knees went weak.

Debby Giusti is an award-winning Christian author who met and married her military husband at Fort Knox, Kentucky. Together they traveled the world, raised three wonderful children and have now settled in Atlanta, Georgia, where Debby spins tales of mystery and suspense that touch the heart and soul. Visit Debby online at debbygiusti.com, blog with her at seekerville.blogspot.com and craftieladiesofromance.blogspot.com, and email her at Debby@DebbyGiusti.com.

Books by Debby Giusti

Love Inspired Suspense

Her Forgotten Amish Past
Dangerous Amish Inheritance
Amish Christmas Search
Hidden Amish Secrets
Smugglers in Amish Country
In a Sniper's Crosshairs
Amish Blast Investigation

Amish Witness Protection

Amish Safe House

Amish Protectors

Amish Refuge
Undercover Amish
Amish Rescue
Amish Christmas Secrets

Visit the Author Profile page at LoveInspired.com for more titles.

Amish Blast Investigation

Debby Giusti

LOVE INSPIRED SUSPENSE
INSPIRATIONAL ROMANCE

LOVE INSPIRED® SUSPENSE
INSPIRATIONAL ROMANCE

ISBN-13: 978-1-335-58781-7

Amish Blast Investigation

Copyright © 2023 by Deborah W. Giusti

For questions and comments about the quality of this book, please contact us at CustomerService@Harlequin.com.

Love Inspired
22 Adelaide St. West, 41st Floor
Toronto, Ontario M5H 4E3, Canada
www.LoveInspired.com

Printed in U.S.A.

For where your treasure is, there will your heart be also.
—*Luke* 12:34

This book is dedicated to

Carol Rose

A beautiful woman with a huge heart who not only cares for the aged and infirm but also provides support and encouragement for their families.

God bless you, Carol,
for your compassionate ministry
to those in need.

ONE

Rebecca Klein tucked a wayward lock of hair under her *kapp* and peered out the door of Zook's Amish Bakery, where she worked. She had removed the last batch of morning pastries from the oven more than fifteen minutes earlier and had expected to see Mr. Tuttle waiting outside in his pickup truck when she placed the Open sign in the window.

Ever since he had moved to Mountainside, Georgia, thirteen months ago, the kindly man had always been her first customer on Tuesday mornings, when she made raspberry jelly–filled doughnuts, which he claimed were his favorites. Normally she wouldn't have been overly concerned by his late arrival, except last Tuesday he had seemed unsettled and preoccupied.

Trying to ignore the ominous feeling that something was wrong, she grabbed a damp cloth and wiped the counter, then sighed with relief when the crunch of tires over gravel alerted her to his arrival.

He pulled his red pickup into the lot and braked to a stop. With his gray beard, bushy brows and long hair pulled together at the nape of his neck, Arnie—as he had told her to call him—looked scruffy and dirt-poor. A fact her brother, Daniel, frequently mentioned.

"He's a recluse, for sure," she had to admit. Mr. Tuttle rarely ventured into town and seemed content to hole up in his cabin farther up the mountain, yet no matter what her brother thought about Mr. Tuttle, she saw beneath the scruff to the twinkling eyes and warm smile.

Arnie stepped to the driveway, his adorable beagle, Sadie, at his heels. "Stay here, girl," he told his pup, who dutifully settled on to a swath of grass at the side of the bakery and watched as he entered the shop.

"Morning, Becky."

She smiled at his insistence on using the unaccustomed nickname, which he said fit her.

"You and Sadie are running a bit behind schedule today, *yah*?" She reached for a mug and filled it with the fresh brew.

He chuckled, a deep, throaty sound that made her smile even more. "Sadie and I got a late start leaving the cabin."

She placed two jelly-filled doughnuts and the large mug of coffee on the counter and arranged the cream pitcher and sugar bowl next to his napkin.

"Breakfast smells mighty fine." He inhaled deeply and settled on to the bar stool. "As I've mentioned before, your doughnuts are the best I've ever eaten."

Her face flushed with the praise. "You'll have me filled with pride, which is not the Amish way."

"Nothing wrong with hearing the truth when you do a good job." As was his custom, Arnie scooped two spoonfuls of sugar into his coffee, stirred the hot brew and added cream. He raised the mug, took a sip and smacked his lips. "Best coffee ever."

"It is fortunate the Amish farmers do not come for coffee before midmorning. They would say this job and especially your kind words are causing my head to swell."

"I don't understand the Amish way of ignoring those who do well." He rubbed his beard. "Another thing I don't understand is why young Amish men aren't lined up outside begging to court you."

Her cheeks warmed even more. "I have not yet accepted baptism, which is a problem for some."

Arnie arched a brow. "You're not sure about remaining Amish?"

She shrugged. "I am questioning the direction of my life."

"An excellent baker and a woman who knows her mind." Arnie chuckled as he bit into the doughnut. "Where did you get that determination, Becky? From your mother?"

"Perhaps. My father said she could be headstrong as well." Becca filled a small ceramic bowl with water. "I have a treat for Sadie, along with a drink."

"Wait—" Arnie held up his hand. "I want to give you something."

He dug in his coat pocket and pulled out a small leather-bound book in a zippered case. "Take this."

She glanced at the embossed cross on the well-worn cover. "Is this your Bible?"

He nodded. "It has everything you need to know within its pages." He pursed his lips and glanced down as if embarrassed by the confusion he, no doubt, read in her gaze. "I'm going out of town and wanted to ensure you had the Bible before I left."

She raised her brow. "You're leaving Mountainside?"

"Only for a few days."

Glancing at the sweet puppy outside, she asked, "What about Sadie?"

"She'll go with me."

"And your cabin?"

He pulled in a breath. "If something happens—"

A thread of concern tangled along Becca's spine. "What are you saying?"

Arnie held up his hand. "I'm not expecting any problems, but—"

He pushed the Bible into her hands. "There's a person I want you to call if I don't come back by the end of the week. His name and phone number are written on the inside cover. You'll find a spare key to the cabin taped to the back of the Bible."

She clutched the small book to her heart. "I will pray you return quickly so I do not need to call your friend."

"He's more than a friend. He's my son, although I haven't seen Luke-boy since he was a little tyke."

Becca read the pain in the older man's eyes and the slump of his shoulders as, once again, he stirred his coffee, no doubt thinking of the lost years. "I am worried about your safety."

He offered her a weak smile. "I'll be fine, but remember to contact my son, and don't tell anyone about this conversation. Keep the Bible and Luke-boy's information between us."

"But—"

"One more thing, Becky. It'll come out soon enough. My real name is Andrew Thomas. Folks call me Andy, but again, that's something I'd like you to keep to yourself."

Perplexed by the information he had provided and unsure as to why he had used an alias, she was even more concerned about his well-being.

Arnie—or Andy—glanced out the door, where his dog whined. "Sadie looks like she's ready for that treat. You spoil her, Becky."

"I'll put the Bible in the basket on my bike for safekeeping, and I will do as you ask if you do not return within the week. I will also pray for your safety."

For some unknown reason, a lump formed in her throat and she blinked back tears. She blamed it on her still-raw grief over her father's death five months ago and her own confusion about her future. Yes, she longed to know more about the *Englisch* world, but she also wanted the peace and stability of the Amish life. To say she was conflicted was an understatement.

Steeling her resolve and hoping Andy didn't notice her emotional struggle, she hurried outside and placed the bowl of water on the patch of grass near Sadie. The pup licked at the cool liquid, then wagged her tail and waited patiently as Becca held out the dog biscuit.

"You're a *bravver hund*, a *gut* dog." She handed the dog the treat.

Her bicycle was propped against a nearby tree. She tucked the Bible into the zippered pouch attached to the seat and patted Sadie. The sweet beagle was enjoying her biscuit and continued to wag her tail in gratitude for the treat.

Becca walked back to the bakery and climbed the porch steps, still heavyhearted about the information Mr. Tuttle—aka Thomas—had just provided.

A *whoosh* sounded, and a deafening *roar* rocked the bakery. Flames burst through the door, along with a blast of hot air that blew her down the stairs and sent her sprawling onto the gravel lot. For the briefest moment, she smelled the caustic scent of gasoline.

Her heart pounded, and her mouth went dry. She struggled to stand, then, seeing the growing inferno, she stumbled up the stairs. "Arnie! No!"

The wooden structure was engulfed in flames. She reached for the doorknob that was already hot to the touch and yanked it open. Heat enveloped her and sucked the oxygen from around her. She pushed through the entrance, only to be thrown back by another explosion. Windows shattered and shards of glass sprayed through the air.

The owner of the produce store across the street ran toward her. "Becca, are you hurt?"

She grabbed Elizabeth's hand. "Help me save Mr. Tuttle."

"*Ack*, no! He was inside?"

Becca started for the bakery again.

Elizabeth caught her by the shoulders and held her back. "The fire is spreading. There is no way—"

Becca's ears rang from the explosion, drowning out the rest of Elizabeth's statement. The reality of the situation engulfed Becca just as the flames engulfed the one-story wooden bakery. She collapsed into her friend's arms and sobbed. Elizabeth tried to console her, but Becca was overcome with grief and shock as the inferno blazed.

Sirens screamed in the smoke-filled air and drew closer.

Firetrucks from the nearby station, followed by the sheriff's car, pulled into the lot. All around them firefighters unrolled hoses and pumped water on to the blaze.

"Get back," a sheriff's deputy warned.

Elizabeth wrapped her arm tightly around Becca and ushered her toward the produce market. "We will wait in my store."

Still dazed, Becca wiped her eyes, called to Sadie, and both of them followed her friend inside, then huddled near the window. Becca watched in dismay as the firefighters battled the blaze. When the fire was controlled, the door to the store opened.

"Ma'am?" The sheriff touched her arm. "Can you tell me what happened?"

She explained about going outside to give Sadie a biscuit. "An explosion, then fire." The memory swept over her. "I... I tried to save him."

Tears once again burned her eyes.

"Did anything seem abnormal this morning?"

"Abnormal?"

"Did you hear anything unusual or smell anything that might be suspect?"

"I only smelled the pastries I pulled from the oven and the doughnuts that fried on top of the stove."

"A propane stove, correct?"

She nodded. "The appliances run on propane. The tank sits behind the kitchen."

"Has anyone tampered with the tank recently?"

"Tampered?" She shook her head. "Not that I know of. What are you saying?"

"I'm just gathering information. The fire marshal will make the final determination." He jotted a note on a small pad of paper.

"Wait. There is something." She rubbed her forehead. "A whiff of gasoline. Just after the explosion."

He made another notation.

"Did...did you find—" A lump had remained lodged in her throat since the explosion, and her eyes burned from the hot tears that mixed with the acrid smoke in the air.

He nodded as if understanding the question she struggled to ask. "The medical examiner is here. An autopsy will be done." The sheriff rubbed his chin. "Anything you can tell me about the victim?"

"His name is—" She hesitated for a moment. "His name is Arnold Tuttle. He came to the bakery on Tuesday mornings, early. I bake jelly-filled doughnuts." Swiping a hand over her cheek, she added, "Those were his favorite."

"Do you know of any next of kin?"

"He never mentioned a name." She thought of the Bible and what was written on the inside cover that she had promised never to reveal.

The sheriff turned away to answer a query from one of his deputies who had followed him inside. Turning back to her, he asked, "You live with your brother?"

"*Yah*, Daniel Klein. On Lower Mountain Road."

"One of my deputies will take you home."

Becca shook her head. "I have my bike."

"What about your hand, ma'am? It looks like you were burned."

Glancing down, she saw the raised red welt on her palm but felt no pain.

Numb. She was totally numb.

The sheriff continued to talk. His lips moved, but she wondered if she'd remember anything about their conversation when she got home today. All she could think of was Mr. Tuttle.

"The EMTs should look at your hand," the sheriff repeated.

Again, she shook her head. "I must get home. That is, if you have no more questions."

The sheriff pointed her to the door. "I know where to find you if I need additional information."

With Sadie at her heels, Becca hurried outside, eager to escape the stench of burning embers. Her bike had fallen to the ground, most likely during the explosion. She gingerly grabbed the handlebars, righted the bicycle and settled on to the seat.

The ride home had never seemed so long. Her brother was in the distant pasture when she turned into the drive. Sadie trotted behind her. The sweet pup seemed as downcast as Becca felt.

She parked her bike near the barn and unzipped the pouch. Arnie's words played through her mind. *Contact my son.*

Perhaps she should have told the sheriff, although Arnie had asked her to keep the information to herself. Now that he was gone, she wondered if secrecy was still important.

Removing the Bible from her pouch, she let out a soulful sigh and opened the front cover, seeing a name and a number just as he had told her. Two keys were taped to the back inside cover: one the size of a standard door key, and a second one that was much smaller.

Her brother kept a cell phone in the barn for business purposes. She retrieved the cell from his workbench and punched in the number.

"Luke Snyder," a deep voice answered. "How may I help you?"

She pulled in a fragile breath. "My…my name is Becca Klein. A man gave me your name and number this morning. He said I should contact you if something happened to him."

"Is this a prank phone call?" He sounded angry.

"I wish it were so, but Arnie Tuttle told me to call you if—"

"Look, lady, I don't know anyone by that name. Next time, think what you're doing before you play your manipulative games."

"But…it is not a game." Realizing she needed to use Arnie's real name, she rephrased the question. "Do you recognize the name Andy Thomas? He said…he said Luke-boy was his son."

"What?"

Perhaps Andy had imagined his connection to the confused man on the other end of the line.

Becca was confused as well.

"Did you say 'Luke-boy?'"

"*Yah*, this is what he told me. His son, Luke-boy."

"Why didn't Mr. Thomas call me himself?"

"Sir, I hate to tell you—" The words lodged in her throat. Her eyes burned. She had cried so much.

"Are you still there?"

"*Yah*, I am here, but I must tell you—"

"Tell me what?" he demanded.

"Andy Thomas is dead."

Luke checked his GPS before he turned on to the two-lane road that angled off the main highway. The drive from Kentucky had taken longer than he had expected, no doubt because he had skirted the interstate and traveled on the back roads that snaked through the peaceful countryside. As nice as the drive had been, the real beauty of the trip was the last stretch in the North Georgia mountains. He breathed in the crisp, fall air and reflected on the phone call yesterday that had brought back memories of his childhood.

In his mind's eye, he saw the bigger-than-life man who was his father—tall, with piercing green eyes, a square jaw and a perpetual frown when Luke's mother was around. That frown instantly vanished when Luke and his dad hiked the trails or fished in the lake not far from their house.

"We make a good pair, Luke-boy," his dad would say with a wink and a chuckle. Luke agreed. His mother didn't. She claimed his father was hard to live with and egotistical, a word Luke had looked up in the dictionary to determine what his mother meant. He'd never seen that side of his father, but his mother said Luke didn't know the reality of their marriage.

When he was ten years old, he came home from school to find his things packed and the suitcases in the car. Later that night, he and his mother left the only home he had ever known.

Not that Luke had wanted to leave. He had wanted to stay with his dad, but his father was at a scientific conference and wouldn't be back for days. Before climbing into the car with his mother, Luke had run to his dad's home office. "Mom's making me go with her," he wrote on the paper he had pulled from his dad's desk drawer. "I don't want to leave you." He folded the note and placed it under the paperweight he had made for his dad in school.

Luke never heard from his father again, which proved, his mother had assured him, that Luke was better off with the new man his mother said would take his father's place.

Eventually Luke believed her.

Now he was driving to an isolated spot in the North Georgia mountains in response to a phone call that had stirred something deep within him. After all these years, it was hard to believe that faint memory from his youth was valid.

The dirt road needed paving, but the beauty of the area with the changing leaves wasn't lost on him. His mother claimed they were city folk, yet he felt a calm serenity in the rolling hills, tall pines and hardwood trees, and the patches of farmland nestled in the valleys.

"Turn right at the fork in the road," the computer-generated voice on his GPS system prompted.

Luke complied, then eased up on the gas, rolled down his window and inhaled a lungful of the cool air.

A clearing appeared.

"Destination on the left," the mechanical voice declared.

He braked to a stop and studied the two-story, white-clapboard Amish home, the nearby barn and assorted outbuildings, and dirt drive surrounded by pastures of grazing cattle, sheep and goats, along with a half dozen horses fenced in a nearby paddock.

A windmill turned in the breeze, probably drawing water to supply the home and barn. The smell of animals and hay mixed with the pungent whiff of fertilizer and the loamy scent of red Georgia clay.

He glanced again at the address he had scribbled on a notepad. The woman had introduced herself as Becca Klein. He hoped to find her at home and wondered what he would do if his trek had been in vain.

Slowly he eased his pickup through the gate and braked to a stop by the side of the barn. The turning leaves and chill in the air spoke of the encroaching winter.

He stepped from his car and eased the door closed, not wanting to disturb the tranquility of the bucolic scene that spread before him.

Pulling in a deep breath, he headed with determined strides to the house, climbed the porch stairs and rapped twice on the door. Blue curtains on a nearby window pulled back ever so slightly. No doubt, someone was checking to see who had come to call.

He removed his baseball cap, raked his free hand through his hair and waited for the door to open.

Blue eyes. He pulled in a breath and lost himself for a moment in the crystal clarity of her eyes and the sorrow that rimmed them.

Her golden hair was pulled back into some type of a bun covered by a crisp white covering. A few wayward strands had escaped her careful coiffure and tangled around her earlobes and onto her cheeks that warmed into a peach glow as her eyes widened and her mouth opened ever so slightly. She glanced over her shoulder before she stepped outside and closed the door behind her.

He moved back, giving her room, lest the strange feelings washing over him were reacting within her as well.

"You're Luke." Her voice was soft and smooth with a melodious lilt.

He nodded. "You…you called me yesterday."

Silly response on his end. Of course she had called him, or he never would have been hovering on her doorstep feeling like a tongue-tied teen.

It wasn't a feeling Luke knew or wanted. Disheartened by his confusion, he squared his shoulders and slapped his hat against his leg. "I'm not sure why I came here. Evidently I want more information about the man who died."

Her lashes fluttered as her gaze dropped momentarily. "It is hard to lose a father."

"Look, ma'am, I won't pretend to have any feelings for the person who claimed to be my father, and I'm not even sure the man who died was related to me. Andy Thomas hasn't been in my life for the last fifteen years."

"I am sorry." The sincerity of her words as well as the pain that flashed from her gaze made him regret the coldness of his statement.

He glanced at the farmhouse and swallowed down the concern that bubbled up within him. He didn't know Becca Klein, and he had left his home in Kentucky without telling anyone. The secrecy about his spur-of-the-moment trip, which he'd thought was important yesterday, gave him pause. If anything happened to him, no one would ever know his whereabouts. He would simply disappear, just like his father had done. At least that's what the news app on his phone and the story in the papers had reported thirteen months ago when Andrew Thomas had left the research facility in Tennessee where he worked.

"I'm not sure about any of this," he said, hoping to drive home his frustration.

"*Yah*, it is strange, for certain, but so was your father's death."

A beagle peered around the edge of the house, then barked a greeting and bounded toward Luke.

Unable to hide his pleasure in seeing the playful pup, he leaned down and caressed the dog's neck. "You're a friendly guy."

"He's a she," the woman corrected. "Her name is Sadie, and she appears to recognize you."

Luke continued to pat the dog. "I've never seen her before."

"Sadie was your *datt*'s dog."

"But I told you I've never seen her."

"Perhaps not, but Sadie's warm welcome proves it."

"Proves what?" He was confused.

"Although years younger, you look exactly like your *datt*."

Suddenly Luke couldn't take the swell of emotion that overcame him. He didn't want to know anything more about a father who had deserted him, and he didn't believe the man his mother had painted in a negative light would become friends with an Amish woman. A very pretty Amish woman, at that.

He pulled in a breath and steeled his jaw. "I don't doubt what you're saying, but I'm not ready to learn anything more about the man who abandoned me. It was a mistake to come here."

Luke turned on his heel and headed to his truck. He refused to glance back at the woman on the porch as he pulled on to the road and accelerated. As he was rounding the first turn, a black sedan raced much too fast around the bend. He laid on his horn to warn the erratic driver who had crossed over the yellow line to get into his own lane.

As the sedan sped away, Luke glanced at his rearview mirror. What he saw tugged at his heart.

Sadie, the friendly beagle, was running after Luke's red truck.

TWO

Becca's heart pounded with regret after Luke's pickup disappeared from sight. She had notified Andy's son of his passing, never expecting Luke would reject her outreach. Overcome with sadness that the meeting had not gone well, she glanced around the barnyard, looking for Sadie.

"Where are you, girl?" She started for the barn, thinking the pup could be inside, sniffing at bales of hay. Before she stepped into the dark interior, a black car with tinted windows pulled into the drive.

A big man—probably six-two and well over two hundred pounds—stepped from the car. He had a shaved head that accentuated his round face and was dressed in a dark fleece jacket, jeans and work boots. From the bulge on his hip, he appeared to be carrying a weapon.

Perhaps he was law enforcement, but she didn't see a badge.

Becca squared her shoulders and washed any sign of emotion from her face in hopes of deterring the visitor from feeling welcome. "Is there something you need?"

The guy eyed her with a narrow gaze and took a step forward. She didn't like his arched brow or the sneer on his full face.

"You're that girl from the bakery. Becca Klein."

She glanced at a distant pasture, wishing her brother was nearby. She also wished Luke hadn't left. Not that she would rely on him to protect her yet having another person in the area would soothe her nerves.

"I need to ask you a few questions." The guy stepped closer. Closer than she wanted him to be.

"I answered the sheriff's questions yesterday." She took a step back. "You can talk to him if you are law enforcement."

He chuckled, a raspy sound that made her flesh prickle. "Look, lady, I know you and Arnold Tuttle were friends. Someone in town said he often stopped by the bakery. I'm wondering what you two talked about, and if he mentioned any special papers or information he wanted you to keep for him."

"I served him doughnuts and coffee at the bakery. We did not discuss anything else."

"Now, come on, little lady. A guy who's holed up in a mountain cabin probably had a lot to get off his chest."

She wasn't sure how the man knew about Andy's cabin.

"Who are you?" she demanded.

"A friend."

The man in work boots didn't appear to be a friend of her compassionate customer who offered compliments and affirmation.

Jutting out her jaw, she nodded ever so slightly. "As I mentioned earlier, the sheriff should be able to help you."

He leaned closer. "I'm not interested in the sheriff. I'm interested in what you can tell me." He grabbed her arm.

She tried to jerk free of his hold. "You're hurting me."

He raised his brow. "Am I? Then maybe you'll tell me what you know about Mr. Tuttle."

"I don't know anything."

He tightened his grip.

She gasped. "Get in your car and leave this farm. Now!"

He twisted her arm behind her back. His free hand closed around her throat. "Let's go over this again. You were going to tell me where Mr. Tuttle kept his papers. Or maybe he mentioned computer files or an external hard drive."

"The Amish do not have computers, so I do not know what you are talking about."

He leaned close to her ear. "What *do* you know about? He had to have told you something."

She remained silent.

He tightened his grip. "Come on, lady. Talk."

But she couldn't talk, because his hand blocked her windpipe. She tried to scream. The effort took more air than she could muster. Her head spun, and her lungs burned. Her knees went weak.

The sound of an approaching car made her fear the big guy with the shaved head had a partner. Tires crunched on the dirt drive. A door slammed.

She swung her foot, hitting his shin.

"Stop it." He breathed into her ear, then pulled her toward the barn. Her heart nearly stopped, thinking of what he would do with her there.

She struggled to free herself. Footsteps approached in a flurry of motion. The glare from the sun blinded her.

The attacker released his hold. She collapsed, her face to the ground, and gasped for air. The sounds of a scuffle above her, along with grunts and groans, made her heart beat even faster.

Heavy footfalls raced away.

The roar of a vehicle backing on to the main road and the screech of tires as it accelerated made her tremble all the more, wondering who had left her and who had stayed behind.

"Tell me you're okay." A man's voice.

She glanced up. The sun continued to blind her, and she couldn't see his face. Lifting her hand to block the glare, she stared into green eyes and blond hair, a square jaw and the rugged complexion of the man who had come to her rescue.

Relief fluttered over her.

Whether her rescuer was willing to admit the truth or not, she knew the man peering down at her was Andy Thomas's son.

"You came back, Luke. Just in time."

"Are you okay?" Luke asked again, concerned about her pale face and drawn brow.

"*Yah*, I… I am not hurt."

"Can you stand?" He placed his hand around her arm and helped her to her feet. "Who was that guy?"

"I… I thought he was law enforcement—until he attacked me."

She brushed the dirt from her apron and dress and motioned Luke toward the house. He followed her into the kitchen and breathed in the smell of the biscuits and bacon she had, no doubt, prepared earlier this morning.

The kitchen was cast in shadow. Working quickly, Becca pulled back the curtains, then opened the woodstove and added a log.

"The coffee will take only a few minutes to heat." She washed her hands at the sink, then moved the half-filled pot to the front burner and pointed Luke to the table. "Sit, please. Would you like something to eat?"

He shook his head. "I ate on the road, but coffee sounds good."

Sadie whined at the door. "Mind if I let her into the house?" he asked. "She brought me back to you."

Seeing the question in Becca's gaze, he explained about spying the dog in his rearview mirror. "I pulled to the side of the road, opened the door and she hopped into the truck. I thought taking her back to you would have been my good deed for the day. Little did I know you were in danger."

"Then Sadie deserves a treat for her actions. I keep dog food on hand for the strays that stop by the farm at times." Becca pulled a dog biscuit from her pantry and handed Luke a small bowl. "Fill this with water in case she wants a drink."

The pup appreciated the water, drank her fill and then sat dutifully next to Luke as she chewed on the biscuit.

Becca poured the heated coffee into two cups and placed them on the table, along with the sugar bowl, cream pitcher and a spoon.

Slipping into a chair, Luke added two spoonfuls of sugar and a dollop of cream to his coffee. He took a long draw of the hot brew and eyed her for a moment. "Do you have any idea what the man wanted?"

"He thought Andy had given me papers or computer files. I told him I didn't have anything of your father's."

"But you did have my name and phone number."

"Which was written in his Bible." She explained again about his father's request that she contact Luke. "He said he was leaving the area for a few days, and if he didn't return, I was to contact you. That was just minutes before the explosion."

"It sounds as if he expected something might happen to him. Did the fire marshal determine what caused the blast?"

"I have not seen anyone from the fire department

today, so I do not know what was discovered. If you want to talk to the marshal, we could go to town."

"Is that where Andy lived?"

She shook her head. "He had a cabin farther up the mountain."

"Can you give me directions?"

"It is better if I show you. The roads are not named, and the cabin is difficult to find."

"You wouldn't mind?"

"We can go as soon as we drink our coffee."

He took another sip. "I had shoved all thoughts of my childhood from my mind. Then I got your phone call."

"Your father loved you."

Luke frowned. "How can you say that?"

"I saw it in his eyes when he talked about you. A man can hide many things, but not love for his child."

The clip-clop of a horse's hooves on the paved road caught Luke's attention, followed by the squeak of a buggy turning on to the gravel drive.

Luke stood just as the door opened.

An Amish man—twenties, tall and lanky—stepped into the kitchen and scowled at Luke, then glanced at Becca. "What is this?"

Luke rounded the table and extended his hand. "Luke Snyder. I assure you, nothing improper occurred. Your wife was kind enough to provide information about a man's death." He paused for a moment. "A man who may have been my father."

"Daniel is my brother," Becca quickly explained.

Luke's brow raised. "He's not your husband?"

She shook her head. "I am not married."

For some reason, Luke felt a swell of relief, but her brother seemed upset as he pointed to the still-open doorway. "Come outside to the porch, Rebecca, where we can talk privately."

Luke held out his hands apologetically once the brother left the house. "I'm sorry." He glanced at Becca. "I'll find my own way to the cabin."

She shook her head and walked purposefully toward the door. "I will guide you there, but wait here while I talk to Daniel."

With that, she hurried outside, leaving Luke to wonder about the sibling struggle that seemed to be bubbling up between Becca and her brother. If he were a praying man, he would ask the Lord to calm their upset, but he had learned as a little boy crying in his bed that God didn't listen to his prayers. If the Lord hadn't listened to Luke as a confused child grieving the loss of his father, He wouldn't listen to Luke now.

Becca closed the kitchen door behind her and raised her chin with determination.

"I bought a newspaper in town." Daniel unfolded the paper. "Do you see the picture on the front page?"

She glanced at the paper he held out toward her. A knot formed in her stomach. "The burned remains of the bakery."

"*Yah*, that is right, and if you read the article you would realize some people suspect the explosion was due to criminal activity. You don't know what your sweet Mr. Tuttle was involved in." Daniel's eyes narrowed. "I told you this man was not to be trusted."

"Andy was a considerate person. A *gut* man. I will not fall prey to lies about him."

"I thought his name was Arnie."

She sighed. "My mistake."

"I am worried about your safety, Becca. You know

nothing about this man's son, who you invited into the house."

"I'm taking him to his father's cabin. Be reasonable, Daniel."

"You are the one who has a problem being reasonable."

"I do not want to argue."

"Nor do I. That is why I insist you remain here."

"I appreciate your concern, but I will be back in an hour or two."

"Use your head, Becca. This is not some outreach you need in your life now. *Datt* said you were too much of a free spirit. He was right."

She bristled. "*Datt* also said I was impetuous and uncontrollable, because he wanted to control me."

"It is as a father should."

"You don't mean that."

He sighed. "*Control* is the wrong word—you are correct. He wanted to raise you up in the Amish way to love *Gott* and follow the precepts of our faith."

"I love the Lord whether I'm wearing the *kapp* or not, but I wanted freedom to live my life as I felt *Gott* wanted. That was not under the control of my domineering father."

"Nor do you want to be equally yoked to an Amish man," Daniel retorted. "Why are you waiting for baptism? Are you harboring thoughts of leaving the faith?"

She stared at him, unwilling to answer.

"Eli Schwartz," Daniel continued, "has expressed interest in courting you, Becca, but you are too stubborn to see what a *gut* man he is."

"A *gut* man, I agree. But not the man for me."

Daniel rolled his eyes. "What am I to do? I promised *Datt* I would take care of you."

"You can allow me to find my own way and use my own mind to make my own decisions."

He shrugged. "Show this stranger the cabin, but if you do not return before dark, I will go there to ensure you are all right."

Luke stood when she returned to the kitchen. "I know your brother's upset."

She removed Luke's cup from the table and placed it in the sink. "My brother tries to be like my father."

"And your father lives nearby?"

She shook her head. "My father died five months ago of a heart attack. He worked hard and refused to take the medication the doctor prescribed."

"I'm sorry, Becca."

"The Amish claim it is God's will, but my father's stubbornness had something to do with his passing."

"Now you live with your brother."

"*Yah*, but he is courting a lovely lady named Katie, who lives nearby with her *datt* and brother. When they marry, I will need to find my own way."

He glanced at the well-maintained home. "Could you stay here?"

"I could, and he has made the offer, but his new wife needs her own home without a sister-in-law underfoot."

"Where will you go?"

She shrugged. "As the Amish say, *Gott* will provide."

Becca grabbed the small Bible Luke's father had given her off the counter and pointed to the door. "We will go now, before my brother becomes more demanding."

The newspaper lay on the porch rocking chair when they stepped outside, but Daniel was nowhere to be seen. He was probably in the barn or one of the outbuildings. She refused to give in to his request about staying home. Andy had been a friend. She would help his son find his cabin.

Sadie trotted at her side. Becca glanced at Luke. His

square jaw was tight, and his steps determined as they headed to his truck. He stopped at the passenger side and opened the door for her. She appreciated the nice gesture.

"Thank you." She climbed onto the seat and buckled her seatbelt.

Sadie hopped into the rear.

"How're you feeling?" Luke pointed to her bandaged hand once he settled behind the wheel.

"A small burn from yesterday, but thanks to your help today, I am fine." She gingerly touched her neck.

He leaned closer. She smelled his earthy aftershave. "You already have a mark forming, Becca. The sheriff should be notified about this guy."

"I made a mistake thinking he was law enforcement, which I will not do again."

Luke started the engine and pulled out of the drive. "I doubt law enforcement would use such tactics. You said he wanted information."

"He thought I knew about your father's papers and computer files."

Luke glanced at her momentarily before he turned his gaze back to the road. "Did Andy give you anything?"

"Only the Bible." She pointed to where she had placed it on the console. "I'm sure he wanted you to have it."

Luke held up his hand as if to stop her train of thought. "I'm not religious."

"Perhaps if you read the Bible, you would find new meaning to your life."

"I'm doing well without Scripture, Becca. I'm studying regenerative farming and trying to accrue my own stock of non-GMO seeds."

His comment surprised her. "You are a farmer?"

"More of a horticulturist. I raise produce and harvest the seeds in hopes of saving many of the plants that have been genetically modified. My mother is gluten-intolerant, and some scientists believe altering wheat over the years has led to a higher gluten content, which has increased gluten intolerance within the population."

His concern for his mother's condition proved Luke had a big heart, although he tried to be stoic about his father's death. The loss of a loved one—even if the relationship had been flawed—was always hard. She knew that all too well after her own father's death. Her *datt* had been a difficult man, but he was still her father, and she grieved his passing. Luke would grieve as well, whether he allowed his pain to surface or not.

Andy had helped her when her father had died. The least she could do was help his son. Then she thought of the man who had accosted her earlier. Would he return, and if so, would he try to do her harm?

THREE

Luke attempted to remain unaffected by everything that had happened in the last twenty-four hours, but the phone call from Becca had unsettled him even though he tried not to show his upset.

Her comment about being called "Luke-boy" had been like a knife to his heart. The memories of the man he had idolized as a child had bubbled up anew, jarring him to the quick. He didn't want to admit the reality even to himself, but he had always longed to renew his relationship with his dad.

If only he hadn't pushed aside his true feelings in his childhood. No doubt his allegiance to his mother played into it. He hadn't wanted to hurt her by returning to the man she said was insensitive to her needs. As a child, Luke had been a mixed-up little boy who longed for his father, but he was swayed by his mother's hateful rhetoric about her ex. No child should have to decide between two parents when he loved both and didn't understand the very adult situation of their marriage's breakup.

"How old were you when your parents divorced?" Becca asked as if reading his thoughts.

"I was ten. My mother claimed Andy was difficult to live with. She had evidently gotten involved with another scientist."

"Scientist? I don't understand."

"Andrew Thomas was an acclaimed researcher. He worked at the Tennessee Research Institute and was one of their lead scientists."

"In Nashville?"

Luke shook his head. "The lab's in a remote part of the state about two hour's drive from Nashville. The nearest town is Waterbend."

"That's where you lived?"

"Actually we lived on the grounds of the Institute. The leading researchers were provided homes. Looking back, I wonder if the isolation was difficult for my mother. She enjoyed city life, with plays and concerts and shopping. As an extrovert, she longed for an active social life, which wasn't part of the rural Tennessee lifestyle Andy seemed to enjoy."

"What did your father research?"

Luke shrugged. "My mother never talked about his work, so I don't know. Some years ago, after I moved out of my adoptive father's house, I tried to find information about the Institute. The only thing I could uncover was that it was a prestigious facility."

"If your *datt* was a leading scientist, why would he move to Georgia and hole up in a mountain cabin?"

"All I know is that he disappeared a little over a year ago. I found mention of it in a few news reports."

"So the papers and files the guy with the bald head wants could involve the laboratory where Andy worked?"

"That's a likely conclusion."

"We are almost to the cabin," Becca said, her voice filled with some of the confusion he was feeling. He appreciated her help, but he didn't want her harmed by anyone seeking information about Andrew Thomas.

"Take the fork in the road to the right," she instructed.

He pulled in a breath and followed her directions, his eyes on the thickly forested area lining the road.

"How did Andy find this cabin?"

"The land was owned by a family in town. They had used it as a hunting cabin and decided to sell it when their sons, who enjoyed hunting, married and moved away from the mountain."

"You've been here before?".

"I surprised your dad last year. He told me his birthday was approaching, so I made a batch of the jelly-filled doughnuts he enjoyed and delivered them." She smiled sweetly, as if the memory warmed her heart. "He was surprised and seemed to appreciate the gesture."

"He must have liked you."

"He liked the doughnuts and coffee and having someone to talk to."

She chuckled, causing Luke's chest to tighten. There was something about Becca that tugged at his heart. He blamed it on the news she had shared about his long-lost father.

"Your *datt* was affirming and thoughtful," she continued. "He was grateful for the smallest gesture and for any kindness shown to him. In return, he offered advice and wise counsel, which I appreciated."

"My mother had less flattering words to say about him."

Becca nodded. "Yet you have *gut* memories that have sustained you over the years."

After he and his mother had left Tennessee, Luke had clung to the memories. With time, he had replaced them with his mother's perspective and had eventually agreed to be adopted by his stepdad. Perhaps he had been wrong to allow her to sway the reality of his past.

"That leads to the cabin." Becca pointed to a dirt path through the thick vegetation.

He made the turn and eased his speed, expecting a shack to appear in the midst of the thick vegetation. Instead, the road led to a grassy knoll where a hand-hewn cabin sat on the side of the hill and looked down on to a pristine valley with a rocky stream ambling through a meadow of lush grass.

His breath hitched as he braked to a stop and took in the massive porch, large picture windows and two-story log home, the immaculate landscaping, sturdy porch furniture and well-kept lawn. A vegetable garden sat on the far side of the house, and a small flower garden edged the side of the front lawn.

"It's not what I expected."

Becca patted his hand. "Your father wanted people to believe he was a recluse, but as I told you, he was a *gut* man. It looks like he made a lot of improvements to the property since I was here, and you can tell he cared for the cabin and surrounding land."

Luke sat for a long moment before he opened his door. Sadie jumped out and ran to a smaller flower garden some twenty feet from the cabin, where an Adirondack chair sat. She sniffed the chair and whined, then dropped to the grass and rested her head on her paws.

"Your father told me he liked to sit there and watch the valley." She pointed to the beautiful scene that panned out below them.

Luke turned to take in the view. His breath caught as he stood in awe of the pristine landscape. In the distance, he saw deer grazing, and a gaggle of geese flew overhead in V formation. Here a man could be one with nature, which had always been Luke's dream.

Now he wondered if he truly *was* his father's son.

* * *

Becca removed the larger of the two keys from the back of the Bible. "I'll open the door in case you want to go inside."

She left him on the lawn, climbed the stairs to the front door and glanced back at Luke, who remained near the flower garden, seemingly spellbound by the view, before she slipped the key into the lock and turned the knob.

After opening the door, she stepped into the dark interior, inhaling the light scent of the wood fireplace and beeswax from the two tall candles that sat atop the table.

Again, she glanced back to check on Luke.

A rustle sounded from behind the door. Her heart pounded a warning as a large form pushed her to the floor. The door slammed shut, and the man flipped the lock. She glanced up to see a huge presence dressed in dark clothing. The same man who had attacked her earlier.

She screamed.

Footfalls sounded on the porch.

"Becca!" Luke pounded on the door.

Sadie barked.

The man dropped to his knees beside her. "Where are they? Where are the files?"

Her breath caught. She shook her head. "I don't… I don't know about any files."

He grabbed her throat, just as he had done near her barn.

She scratched his face.

He swatted her hand away and slapped her across the jaw. She groaned, her vision swayed and her stomach roiled from the blow.

Luke continued to pound on the door. "Becca." His footfalls retreated.

Don't leave me, she inwardly cried.

The man jerked upright, kicked her in the abdomen and raced to the rear door. She moaned and stumbled to her feet. He ran headlong into Luke and punched his fist into his jaw, aiming a second blow at his gut. Luke gasped, doubled over, then righted himself. The bald man took off running into the dense forest. Luke started after him. Sadie raced past him and barked as she charged after the assailant.

A series of shots fired.

Becca staggered to the door. "No," she screamed, anxious about Sadie's and Luke's well-being.

"Please, *Gott*, protect them."

She stumbled outside, seeing nothing. Her heart nearly stopped, fearing they both were dead.

FOUR

Luke lost sight of the attacker. Frustrated, he turned back to the cabin and whistled for Sadie. "Come here, girl."

Relieved when the pup appeared through the brush, he rubbed her neck, then motioned toward the cabin. "We need to check on Becca."

He found her on the back porch, leaning against the banister. A handprint was outlined on her pretty cheek, and a small cut above her eye was seeping blood.

Racing to her side, he wrapped his arm around her slender waist and helped her into the cabin. After he settled her on to the couch, he locked both the front and back doors, then dampened a kitchen hand towel.

"You're hurt," he said, returning to her side. He handed her the towel, which she dabbed against her cut.

"I was more surprised than anything."

She was making light of the attack. He could see the pain in her eyes and the way her shoulders drooped as she gingerly held the cool cloth against her forehead.

"Did you recognize the man?"

She nodded. "It was the bald man who attacked me this afternoon at the farm. Both times he grabbed my neck." She thought back to the newspaper article her brother had showed her and the bald man's demand for Andy's papers and files. "Do you have any idea what your father was involved in, Luke?"

He sighed. "As I mentioned, he worked in a lab in Tennessee. The government was interested in his research, but everything was top secret—at least, that's how it seemed to me whenever I tried to find information about his work."

"He came here a little over a year ago. Why would he leave Tennessee?"

"I… I don't know."

Becca wondered if Luke was holding something back from her. She thought of her brother's concern about going to the cabin with Andy's son. Had he been right to warn her?

She stared into Luke's green eyes that looked identical to his father's. Was Andy Thomas involved in something suspect, and if not, why had someone broken into the cabin?

Glancing around the living area, she realized a number of the drawers had been pulled open, and papers and books lay scattered on the floor. The man who had attacked her had been looking for something, and she and Luke had interrupted him.

"We should finish searching the cabin in case he missed something," she suggested. They needed clues to what the man was searching for and why he kept insisting she had what he wanted. Otherwise, Becca feared, he might continue to come after her.

As Becca returned the scattered items to their rightful place, Luke peered into the main bedroom. The bed was neatly made. Both the nightstand and dresser were clear. He opened the closet and touched the hanging shirts and two pairs of jeans before he returned to the living area.

"No desk, and I don't see a laptop. Nothing that would have been of interest to someone searching for papers or computer files."

She glanced at the stairway. "Maybe he had an office on the second floor."

"I'll check it out." Luke hurried up the stairs, taking them two at a time. He checked the smaller bedrooms and returned to the kitchen, where Becca was peering into the various cupboards and pantry. "The upstairs looks untouched," he told her. "My guess is we arrived before the big guy finished searching the downstairs."

"The kitchen looks untouched as well." She pointed to the door. "Maybe Andy kept his papers in the outbuilding."

"I hope we find something." Luke hesitated a moment and then added, "Thank you for helping me, Becca. You're a kind person."

She stepped toward the door, but he noticed the tears that filled her eyes and how she wiped them away with the flick of her hand.

He had said something that had upset her. Was it because he mentioned her kindness? He knew the Amish were not big on praise so perhaps his comment had been unsettling. He would have to tread carefully with Becca to ensure he didn't bring her to tears again.

He'd never dated much, and he usually felt somewhat awkward around women, but Becca was different, and it wasn't because she was Amish. She had an inner peace that he'd sensed the first time he had seen her, as if she knew who she was and what she wanted in life. Luke had spent the last few years trying to find purpose to his life. His work with non-GMO seeds had been satisfying, but there was something missing. Being with Becca made him forget that hole in his heart, which he didn't understand. Was it finding information about Andrew Thomas that changed his mind-set? Or was it Becca's melodious voice and understanding gaze? Perhaps it was a bit of both.

Becca grabbed a cluster of keys hanging on a hook by the door before she left the cabin. Luke's comment about her being kind had reminded her of his father. Andy had made a point of mentioning her strengths and attributes, which had always taken her by surprise. She paused to think back over her life and realized she could never recall her own father uttering a compliment or even acknowledging any of her accomplishments, whether it was maintaining the garden and single-handedly canning all the produce after her mother's death or helping in the fields at harvest and keeping up with her much more muscular brother. Daniel had appreciated her help, but her father had said nothing to her, although he had mentioned Daniel's ability and effort.

Pride! Or *hochmut*, as the Amish said. Becca never should have gotten used to Arnie's comments, nor should she be taken by his son.

She led the way to the small freestanding building situated about ten feet from the cabin. She unlocked the door and stepped inside, smelling the pungent scent of freshly cut wood and sawdust. A long workbench sat against a rear wall. Hand tools hung on pegboard above the bench and along the shelving on the side wall. "From the looks of these tools, Andy must have enjoyed woodworking."

"Seems he was good at everything," Luke added, although she recognized frustration in his voice. "Everything except being a father."

So that was the underlying problem. Hoping to deflect his upset, she pointed to the workbench. Luke rummaged through the drawers. "Not much here other than a few scientific magazines, pens and tablets, and a straight edge and calculator."

"No computer files?"

"None that I see." He glanced at Becca. "Andy was going somewhere. He must have cleaned out his papers, knowing he was leaving."

Luke and Becca locked the woodshed behind them. Becca stared at the pile of stacked wood near the shed along with a fifty-five-gallon metal barrel. "Your father probably burned trash in the barrel."

Together, they peered at the ash and the charred tops of a few boxes. "What's that?" Becca pointed to the edge of a letterhead. Luke plucked it from the barrel, blew the soot off the burned paper and held it up.

She stepped closer. "'McWhorter, Esq.?' Do you recognize the name?"

"*Esquire* indicates he's licensed by the state bar association to practice law. Can you make out the address?" Luke studied the printed letterhead.

"Water something?"

He nodded. "I told you my parents and I lived on the grounds of the Institute located near Waterbend before they divorced."

"Evidently your dad stayed in touch with Mr. Mc-Whorter."

"Who might know why someone is interested in my father's files."

"You could call Mr. McWhorter."

"I could." He pulled out his cell phone and glanced at the screen. "If I had coverage out here. I need to head back to town."

"You might get reception at my house." She glanced

at the dark clouds rolling over the mountain. "A storm is brewing. The road can be treacherous when it's wet."

"Plus, I don't want your brother to worry. After I make the phone call, I'll head back to the cabin and bunk here tonight."

Becca shook her head. "This would not be smart with the bald-headed man on the loose. He could come back searching for more information."

"I can handle him, Becca."

"Hmm." She raised a brow.

"You think I'd be safer at a motel in town?"

"We have a spare bedroom. You can stay with us."

"I doubt your brother would want me to spend the night, especially since I'm not Amish."

She smiled. "Daniel tries to mimic my father in his actions when in reality he has a soft heart. He may be momentarily unsettled by having a houseguest who is not Amish, but when he learns about your work with seeds and whatever type of farming you mentioned, he will realize you have common interests."

"I appreciate your offer, but I'm not sure you're right about your brother."

"One night, Luke. Tomorrow you can decide what you are to do."

He sighed, and something tugged at her heart. Luke's eyes were filled with compassion, like his father's, but she felt different when she stared into his gaze. A warmth she wasn't used to feeling spread along her neck. She had liked Andy, but she felt another sensation when she looked at Luke. Something that made her cheeks heat and her insides tingle.

"Take me home, Luke, and stay the night."

"And what if the bald guy comes back, Becca? He

knows where you live. He's come after you twice and could do so again."

"You and Daniel should be able to protect me. As my mother used to say, there is safety in numbers."

Luke reached out his hand and touched the tender spot on her cheek. His fingers were gentle as they rubbed against her skin, causing heat to grow in her cheeks and around her heart.

"I never want him to hurt you again."

The sincerity in Luke's voice gave her pause. Daniel had been right. She needed to be careful around the *Englischer*, not because he would harm her, but because of the way he made her feel—special, important, valued— feelings she'd never had before.

A rumble of thunder sounded overhead. Luke placed his hand on the small of her back. "Let's hurry to the truck before the rain starts to fall."

He turned and called for Sadie.

The pup scurried after them.

Becca wasn't worried about getting wet, but she was worried about her attraction to this *Englischer* man and the way her heart nearly skipped a beat as he pulled her close and ushered her into his truck.

Luke could be trouble. Not to her well-being, but to her heart.

FIVE

Luke opened the passenger door for Becca, and after she was seated with Sadie at her feet, he rounded his truck and slipped behind the wheel. He glanced once again at the mountain cabin and wondered about Andrew Thomas. Luke's mother had filled his head with so many negative ideas about her ex-husband that Luke didn't know what was real and what was the skewed memory of a child. Growing up, Luke had thought the bigger-than-life man who chuckled as they hiked the trails had been a figment of his imagination. Since Becca's call, he'd realized those memories could have been accurate.

If only he could dig deeper and uncover the truth.

The sky darkened, and rain splattered the windshield. "Your brother will be worried about you."

"I'm often out by myself in storms, and that's usually not a problem."

"Then I'm the deciding factor."

She nodded. "I must admit that Daniel is somewhat cautious around the *Englisch*. No doubt, he let my *datt*'s negative comments sway him."

Luke thought of how his mother had biased his feelings toward his own father. "What about your mother? Was she antagonistic to those who weren't Amish?"

Becca shook her head and smiled. "I never heard my mother say a bad word about anyone, Amish or *Englisch*. She was a wonderful woman who died too young."

"I'm sorry for your loss."

"The Amish talk about *Gott*'s will, and maybe it is so, but I wish she were still with us."

"Was she sick?"

"My *mamm* was never sick. It was an accident. Her sister lives a few hours north of Ethridge, Tennessee, with her husband."

"Ethridge is an Amish community?"

"*Yah.* My mother and my aunt were raised there. My aunt moved to her husband's farm once they were married. My *mamm* boarded a bus to visit them. A storm blew in as they went over the mountain before they could get to the highway."

"There was a bus accident?"

"So many Amish die in buggy accidents, we never think anything will happen on a bus. She was standing in the aisle, talking to another lady, when the driver slammed on the brakes to miss hitting another vehicle on the road. She was thrown against a metal bar near the front of the bus." Lowering her gaze, Becca sat for a long moment, and when she finally spoke, her voice was little more than a whisper. "My mother never regained consciousness."

Luke's heart went out to the sweet woman who carried the pain of her mother's death. He stretched out his right hand and wrapped his fingers through hers. "Death is always hard."

Her pretty blue eyes glistened with tears as she gazed at him. "What about your mother?"

"She travels and spends this time of the year in Italy with my adoptive dad."

"Your adoption is the reason your last name isn't Thomas."

He nodded. "My mother insisted we make a clean break from my dad. I was too young to stand up for myself—plus, I thought Andy would come to get me before the adoption was finalized. When he never appeared, I realized my mother had been right about him all along."

"What about now that you're an adult? Do you see things differently?"

The rain intensified. He turned the windshield wipers to high. "I still wonder why he never contacted me. I understand he was upset with my mother, but I don't know why he was upset with me. As a child, I feared he thought I was complicit with my mother's desire to leave him. I had written him a note, but—"

He glanced at the rearview mirror. "There's a car coming up behind us, Becca. He's driving too fast."

She looked back. "It's hard to see anything in this downpour."

Luke flicked on his hazard lights and slowed his speed. The road bordered a steep incline that could be deadly if the wheels didn't hold the road. "I want to ensure he sees us, especially as fast as he's driving."

Becca grabbed the console and the armrest on the door as if to brace herself. "There's a sharp turn ahead," she warned.

"Is there any spot to pull over so he can pass us?"

"There's a narrow outcrop just after the curve."

The curve appeared ahead. Luke eased up on the gas and tapped the brake as he maneuvered the sharp bend in the road. To the right, the road dropped off into nothing. Without traction, the truck could slip over the edge. Again, he tapped the brake and gripped the steering wheel tighter.

The rhythmic click of the hazard lights and the drum of rain on the roof of his truck filled the cab and made it hard to hear any other sounds.

Becca peered over her shoulder at the approaching vehicle. "The car's drawing closer. Why does he not slow down?"

Luke didn't have an answer. His attention was on the road and the waves of water that washed over the pavement in the blustery wind that had picked up since they'd turned on to the mountain road.

The driver of the car behind them flashed his lights.

"What does he want?" Becca asked, fear edging her voice.

"Maybe for me to pull over, which I'll do at the first opportunity. The driver is endangering himself and both of us."

The narrow turnoff lane appeared ahead. Luke slowed and eased to the side of the pavement, relieved to be off the main road.

Glancing again at the rearview mirror, he saw the black car swerve around them and then pull to a stop. The door opened, and a big man got out. He wore a flannel jacket.

Becca grabbed Luke's hand. "It's the bald man."

The other man reached into his waistband. Luke knew what was coming before he saw the weapon.

Becca gasped.

"Hold on." He jammed the gearshift into Reverse and stepped on the accelerator.

The guy raised his weapon.

"Get down, Becca."

She didn't move. Luke grabbed her shoulder and pushed her head into her lap just as a round exploded. Sadie sat at her feet, shaking.

Luke gripped the wheel with his left hand, jammed the gearshift into Drive and floored the accelerator. The pickup fishtailed out of the turnoff lane and screeched around the sedan.

The bald guy fired two more rounds. One hit the running board.

"Stay down," Luke warned again.

Placing both hands on the wheel, he steered along the narrow mountain road, going much too fast. The rain eased somewhat, but the road was slick, and anything could happen to send them over the edge.

The sedan would catch up to them before long, and if they couldn't find a way off the mountain road, they wouldn't be able to elude the big man a second time.

"We need a detour."

Becca raised her head. "The Gingerich farm is not far. There's a pasture on the left with an old barn where they store hay. If we make it there before the black sedan comes around the last turn, we can hide in the barn."

Luke nodded, understanding her strategy. "How far off the road is the barn?"

"About twenty yards. There's a dirt path that winds from the road to the barn. I do not think the bald man will even notice the structure. He will believe we are heading straight down the mountain."

Luke hoped she was right.

He flicked his gaze to the rearview mirror, relieved that the sedan was not behind them. At least not yet.

"Turn there." Becca pointed to the small dirt road that appeared to be little more than a trail through the field. "We've got to get inside the barn."

Luke eased his truck along the path. When he drew closer to the structure, Becca jumped out and ran to open the doors. The old barn listed, and its interior was filled with bales of dried grass that would feed the farmer's livestock throughout the winter. Luke angled into the dark interior, relieved that his truck fit. He killed the ignition and jumped down to help Becca close the doors. Peering through a crack in the wood, he spied the black sedan racing past the dirt path. The car accelerated even faster and headed along a stretch of straight roadway, then eased into another turn and disappeared from sight.

Becca sighed with relief. "He sped past without seeing us."

She turned to Luke. He wrapped his arm around her and pulled her into his embrace. "I'm not sure we could have outrun him if you hadn't told me about this barn."

He could feel her trembling and rubbed his hand over her shoulders. "It's okay, Becca. We're safe."

The barn door creaked. Becca grabbed Luke's hand and held it tight. He stepped protectively in front of her, fearing the bald-headed man had come back for them.

"What is this?" a deep voice bellowed.

Becca's heart had nearly stopped as the door opened, but when the man spoke, she paused for a moment, trying to recognize the voice.

Peering around Luke's strong arms, she let out a sigh of relief. "Mr. Gingerich. It is Rebecca Klein."

"*Ack*, Becca. What are you doing in this old barn, and with this *Englisch* man?"

The question in his voice made her blush. "We were hiding from another man who was chasing us down the mountain."

She introduced Luke. "You probably heard about Mr. Tuttle, who died in the bakery explosion." She pointed to Luke. "This is his son."

Mr. Gingerich shook his head. "A terrible tragedy. Your *datt* lived not far from here, up the mountain."

Luke nodded. "Yes, sir. Becca took me to his cabin, but the man who chased us had broken in and seemed to be searching for something."

The Amish farmer threw his hand into the air. "What is happening these days? A bad element seems to be moving to the area. I am sorry about your father's death and concerned about this man who came after you."

"He passed by," Becca explained, "but we'd like to remain hidden for a short time until we're sure he's not anywhere nearby."

"You will come to the house. Katie is there. You can stay for dinner."

"That is so nice of you, but Daniel will be worried if I do not return home."

He wagged his finger. "You must be careful and tell Daniel to be as well if this man is in the area. Lock your doors." He glanced at the beagle that peered through the passenger window. "The dog will keep watch. A beagle is a *gut hund* and will let you know if anyone ventures on to your property."

"I'll remind Daniel that we must be careful."

The old man peered outside. "The rain has stopped. If you follow the path through the field, you will get to the back road."

"It leads close to our farm," Becca explained. "It is doubtful the bald man would find it. I feel certain he will stay on the main road."

The barn door creaked open, and Katie stepped inside. "Becca, this is a surprise."

Her father explained what had happened, and Becca introduced Luke to her future sister-in-law.

"We'll leave now, but I'll tell Daniel you said hello."

"If anything else happens, you, Daniel and Luke

could spend the night here," Mr. Gingerich said. "There is room, and you would be safe with us."

"Thank you for the offer. I'll mention it to Daniel, but I doubt he would want to leave the farm and his livestock untended." After saying goodbye, Becca and Luke climbed into the truck and pulled out of the barn.

Mr. Gingerich raised his hand in farewell. "Keep close watch and remember to lock your doors."

"They're nice people," Luke said once they headed along the pasture road.

"Katie will make a *gut* wife for Daniel. If you see them together, you will realize they are very much in love."

Luke glanced at her, and she felt her cheeks warm. If only her body didn't reveal her feelings. She had never been in love and wondered if Luke had a girlfriend at home. It would be too intrusive to ask him, and she didn't want to know the answer if he did have a special someone. Instead, she would believe he was not courting anyone, not that she was interested in Luke. Besides, he was *Englisch*, and *Englisch* and Amish did not mix. Yet she could learn more about the *Englisch* way of life with him, which would help her make her decision about seeking baptism. At twenty-two, she was running out of time. The bishop had encouraged her to set a date, but something was stopping Becca.

Perhaps she hadn't chosen baptism yet so she could help Luke. As an unbaptized woman, she had more freedom. Plus, now that the bakery was destroyed, she didn't have a job and had time to help him determine the truth about his father. Although she didn't know if Luke wanted her help.

She directed him on to the narrow back road, knowing that Daniel would be worried about her. She needed to be strong and not succumb to his control. Daniel was a *gut* brother, but he was too protective, although she appreciated his concern.

Glancing at Luke, she said a silent prayer that both men would get along this evening. Luke would not remain in Mountainside for long, but she did not want Daniel's lack of hospitality to send him away before he was ready. Luke had mentioned leaving in the morning. For some reason, that made Becca sad.

Luke drew in a deep breath when he turned into the Klein farm, knowing Daniel would most likely be upset to see him again. Once he learned of the bald man's second attack on Becca, the protective brother would be even more unsettled. The Amish were peace-loving people, but Daniel was worried about his sister and had let his true feelings show earlier today. Luke had no doubt that those same feelings would surface again.

"Pull into the barn," Becca suggested. "We do not want the bald man to know we have returned to the farm."

Luke glanced around. "What about Daniel?"

"He might be in one of the distant pastures." She turned toward the fields, then flicked her gaze back to the house as the kitchen door opened and her brother stepped onto the porch. "He evidently was inside."

"Would it be better if I leave now?"

"Absolutely not. You are a guest, and you are welcome to stay the night."

Luke parked his truck, then followed Becca and Sadie out of the barn just as Daniel came down the porch steps.

"You were gone longer than I expected," he said in greeting.

"A man had broken into the cabin and searched through some of the drawers and cabinets. It took time to tidy the upheaval."

Daniel stepped closer. "There is a bruise forming on your cheek, Rebecca."

"The man pushed past me as he left the cabin and caused me to fall." She touched the spot he indicated. "It is nothing serious."

Her brother glanced at Luke. "Why is this man interested in your father's affairs?"

Luke shook his head. "I don't know, but it's something I need to investigate. I'm sorry that I brought trouble to your sister."

Becca raised her hand. "Remember, your father and I were friends long before I knew he had a son. You did not bring the problem here, and even if you had, the man is in the wrong. You are not."

She straightened her shoulders and turned to Daniel. "We stopped at the Gingerich farm and talked to Katie's *datt*. He invited us to spend the night if you are worried about our safety."

Daniel raised his brow. "Why would you bring Katie's family into this?"

Luke could see Becca's face sour and knew she didn't want her brother to know about their run-in with the bald man on the treacherous mountain road. Luke wouldn't cover up the truth, but he wouldn't provide all the details that could make Daniel even more upset.

"Driving down the mountain, I thought someone was following us and worried it could have been the man who broke into the cabin. A small barn on the Gingerich property provided a chance to hole up until the car passed. We never got a clear view of the driver."

He pointed back to the barn. "Now that Becca is safely home, I can get back on the road."

Daniel pursed his lips and glanced at Becca before turning to Luke. "My mother prided herself on welcom-

ing people to our home. I need to follow her example.
We have a spare room. My sister is a *gut* cook, and we
would be happy to have you stay the night."

"Thank you, Daniel. I appreciate the offer."

Daniel nodded. "Then it is settled." He pointed to the
house. "Please join us."

Luke waited for Becca to lead the way, then he followed her into the kitchen, while Daniel headed to one
of the pastures to check on his horses.

She added wood to the stove and stirred the embers to
ignite the flames. "It is growing late, and I am sure you
are hungry. We will have a light dinner."

"Anything would be fine."

"You are easy to please, like your father, *yah*?"

"I don't know about Andy Thomas's good nature. As
I've mentioned, according to my mother, he was a difficult man."

"A mother should not sway her child against the father."

"And perhaps I should not have taken her words to
heart."

"For a child, this is a hard place to be pulled by two
people you love. I wish you could learn the truth about
your *datt*."

"I respect your opinion, Becca, and the information
you've provided has me questioning what I have believed
about him for so long."

"Then *gut* has come from you being here."

Luke liked Becca's relaxed manner in spite of everything she had gone through. Perhaps it was her Amish
upbringing, but she seemed to accept things as they came
and didn't let problems upset her unduly.

"Thank you for putting me up tonight, Becca. I'll be
out of your hair in the morning."

"You can stay longer, if there is more you need to learn about your father. You might want to talk to the sheriff, and you'll need to decide what to do with the cabin."

"That's why I'm glad about finding the name of the lawyer. I'll call him in the morning."

"Do you think he will have information about your father?"

He nodded. "That's my hope. I should be able to get to Waterbend in about five hours. My mother had a warm and caring woman from town who helped her with her housework. When my parents had social functions, she would babysit me. Even though it's been fifteen years since we lived there, I'll try to find her. She might know something about the lawyer."

The sun was long on the horizon, and the sky was darkening. Luke helped Becca with some of the kitchen chores, and by the time the leftovers were heated and green beans and applesauce were on the table, Daniel came in from the field. He brought the clean scent of the outdoors that made Luke realize how much he enjoyed the mountain freshness and the expansive pastures and rolling hills. Luke wondered if Becca or her brother realized the beauty around them. So often people failed to recognize what they had when they had grown too accustomed to an area.

Later, after they enjoyed the delicious dinner with pie for dessert and Luke helped Becca with the dishes, she poured two mugs of coffee. As if knowing how he liked his coffee, she placed the sugar and cream pitcher on the table and smiled as he ladled the two spoonfuls of sugar and hefty dollop of cream into the cup before heading to the porch. Sadie rose from where she was resting and greeted both of them with licks and nestled close to their legs.

Sitting next to Becca on the porch swing, Luke looked around, taking in the fields and the stars twinkling in the sky. "This is nice, Becca. The land, the mountain as a backdrop, the rolling hills. You have it all here."

She glanced down as if unsure how to respond. "My whole life I have wondered what is beyond this farm and this area. Now you are saying it is all here. I still need to see outside this Amish mountain community for myself."

"Maybe that's how I am about Andrew Thomas. No matter what you tell me—and I do believe you're sincere— I need to uncover the truth about my father for myself."

Becca nodded as if she understood. "We are from different worlds, one plain and the other fancy, yet we are both searching for something. You are searching to know who your father really was, and I am searching to know what life outside the plain world is like. Perhaps we can help each other in our quests."

He looked into her wide eyes and wished he could have more time in this idyllic setting and with this genuine woman who saw beneath the facade and looked into a person's heart. What did she see when she looked into him? Did she see a man trying to find his way in life and uncover his past? Or did she see someone whose values were too far removed from her own?

Becca had a strong faith. Luke put little stock in the spiritual realm. God had abandoned him when he was a child crying himself to sleep. Believing in a higher power was outside his expertise. Becca could have her *Gott*, as she said, and her Amish faith. Luke had to trust himself and what he could uncover on his own, although he envied Becca for what she had here on this small farm. A man could be happy here, especially with a woman like Becca at his side, but Luke needed to face reality. He was leaving tomorrow—leaving the farm and leaving Becca, which made him shake his head with regret.

Morning would come soon enough, and saying good-bye to Becca would be difficult, but he needed to leave before he became too comfortable in this peaceful mountain life. If only Becca knew what she had here. She said he could stay longer than one night, although more time together would bring more complications, which wasn't what Luke wanted.

Before Becca had notified him of Andrew Thomas's death, Luke had been content with his life. Now that he had seen the beauty of the mountain, he knew going back would be hard. Leaving Becca would be even harder.

SIX

Becca enjoyed sitting next to Luke. He was different than the young Amish men in the local area. He was tall and muscular, but his stature was not the main quality that attracted her to him. Instead it was the depth of understanding she saw in his eyes and his desire to help her. Small things like opening the car door and assisting her in the kitchen. Both actions had taken her by surprise and made her wonder if other *Englisch* men would be as considerate. She had to think that Luke was someone special. Sadie had taken to him immediately. Yes, he looked like his father, but dogs could sense a person's mood, and no doubt, Sadie felt secure with the handsome *Englischer*. Becca had to admit that she did as well.

"Would you like more coffee?" she asked when he placed his empty cup on the porch banister.

"I'm fine, thank you, Becca."

"Perhaps another piece of pie?"

The warmth of his smile made her neck tingle.

"You're spoiling me."

"You mean *Englisch* girls don't bake pies for you?"

He laughed. "The *Englisch* girls, as you call them, are more interested in checking their social media and getting their nails done."

She glanced down at her short nails, thinking of how she had chewed them to the nub as a child—much to her father's disapproval.

Luke must have been aware of her feelings, because he touched her arm. "You have pretty hands, Becca."

Once again, he had surprised her with his comment. Her cheeks burned, and she knew if the night hadn't fallen, he would be able to see her blush.

"You are considerate like your father, Luke."

"But I'm not my father."

She nodded. "I didn't mean that you were, but he had a way of making me feel special, which I find in you as well."

He stared at her, and something fluttered in her stomach.

"Are you thinking of Andy Thomas now, or are you thinking of me?" he asked.

"I… I…" She hesitated. "You are the man who is with me."

For a long moment, she stared into his eyes, knowing he understood what she meant. He, too, must sense the draw as they sat together. Although they had only met this morning, she felt content with Luke.

He wrapped his fingers through hers. Her heartbeat increased, and a tingle curled around her neck. Her father's words of warning about being too much in the world played through her mind, but she shoved them aside. Tonight, she wanted to focus on Luke and the way he made her feel, even if she was being foolish. He would leave in the morning, and she would be left on the farm to find her way with only the memories of this night.

She glanced up at him, and time stood still. The farm and the stars overhead faded into the distance, and the only thing she saw was Luke's full lips, lightly parted and drawing ever closer to hers.

The kitchen door creaked open. She jerked and pulled her hand away from Luke's just before her brother stepped onto the porch.

"It is getting late," Daniel announced. "Tomorrow will come early."

Luke must have sensed her brother's concern. He stood and pointed to the barn. "I've got a backpack in my truck that I'll get before I turn in."

Flustered by the sudden change in mood, she stood, feeling the swing brush against her legs. "And I'll take the empty coffee cups to the sink."

She glanced at her brother. "Mr. Gingerich wanted to ensure we locked the doors tonight, Daniel, in case the man at the cabin came back again."

"I'll check the outbuildings," Luke volunteered. "It shouldn't take long."

"Gut." Daniel nodded. "And I will check around the house as well." Daniel headed to the right as Luke started for the barn. He glanced back when her brother was out of sight.

"Thank you for helping me today, Becca, and for sharing what you know about Andy. You put yourself in danger, which I never wanted to happen, but I appreciate all you've done to help me learn more about the man who claimed to be my father."

She hated to hear Luke's comment about Andy's *claim* to being his father. Throughout the day Luke had failed to call Andy his dad. He was still holding back, even after seeing his father's cabin.

If only Luke would stay a few more days, he might be able to accept Andy into his heart. That was her hope, although she knew Luke planned to leave in the morning. Slowly she turned and went into the house, but her thoughts were on the close moment she and Luke had shared on the porch swing. That memory would stay with her for a long time.

Luke pulled his backpack from his pickup and placed it on the porch, then he edged around the outbuildings, the woodpile, the chicken coop and the various small buildings situated on the far side of the barn.

He saw Daniel climb the porch steps and search the darkness. Luke stepped out from the shadows. "I'll check the edge of the forest and see if I hear anything before I come inside."

"Latch the lock behind you." Daniel hesitated a moment before adding, "Thank you for searching the area. We do not usually have people that come on our property at night, but this man seems to be after his own gains."

"Just so he doesn't hurt Becca."

Daniel splayed his arms. "I have tried to do as my *datt* asked, to keep her safe, to steer her in the right direction, but she has a mind of her own, which I am certain you realize. I do not want her to make a mistake about her future."

"She's a grown woman, Daniel, and able to make up her own mind."

"*Yah*, but I do not want her to walk along the wrong path. The Amish stay to themselves and do not mix with the *Englisch*."

Was Daniel trying to warn Luke not to interfere in Becca's life? "I'm leaving tomorrow."

Daniel nodded, as if satisfied with Luke's response. "I will be in the fields early, so if I do not see you before you leave, have a safe trip home."

Home? For so long Luke had felt that he had no home.

The house he and his mother had moved into after she had remarried never seemed like home. Nor did the small ranch house where he lived now.

"Thank you for your hospitality, Daniel. You have a productive farm, and I can tell that you care for the soil and your livestock. In a way, I envy what you have here."

Daniel tilted his head. "I would not think this farm would be of interest to an *Englischer*. Perhaps…it is not the farm that is of interest, but the woman who lives here."

He turned and went into the house, leaving Luke to stare after him. Were his feelings that obvious? He didn't know how he felt about Becca. Was it the farm that made him want to stay, or was it the pretty Amish woman?

Sadie came to rub against his leg. He bent to pet her. "Can you tell I'm confused, girl? I wonder if Andy talked to you when he had problems he couldn't resolve."

He patted the dog. "Let's check that last outbuilding."

As he glanced into the darkened interior of what appeared to be Daniel's workshop, he heard the distant sound of a car's engine. "Come here, girl. Let's stay in the shadows."

Sadie rounded the outbuilding with him and sat at his feet. The sound of the car drew closer.

The entire time he and Becca had been outside, no vehicle had passed by on the road. Now a car was closing in and seemed to be slowing down.

Luke turned his gaze to the house, knowing the kitchen door was unlocked. He wasn't sure where Becca was— hopefully upstairs and away from the windows.

The headlights from the vehicle illuminated the narrow road in front of the farm. The car pulled to a stop. The driver extinguished the headlights and cut the engine.

Luke's pulse pounded as he stared into the night, trying to see through the darkness.

A car stopping on the road at this time of night had to be someone up to no good. The big man with the bald head came to mind.

The car door opened, then eased shut. Footsteps crunched over the gravel drive.

Luke flattened his back against the side of the woodshop and peered around the corner. Pulling out his phone, he tapped in 911 and whispered his need for law enforcement at the Klein farm.

"I'll call dispatch," the operator assured him.

Sadie stood next to him, her ears perked, as if sensing danger. "Shh, girl," Luke soothed.

The footsteps drew closer. A figure appeared in the darkness. The guy stopped for a long moment and stared at the house. Luke followed his gaze. His heart nearly stopped, seeing Becca's sweet face through the kitchen window.

Luke moved away from the woodshop. "I suggest you get back in your vehicle and drive to town if you know what's good for you."

The kitchen door opened. Becca glanced into the darkness, as if trying to discern what was happening outside.

Luke raised his hand in warning. "Shut the door, Becca."

Sadie barked a warning and charged toward the shadowed figure.

Luke tackled the man and knocked him down, then struck him in the gut.

A siren sounded in the distance.

The big guy stumbled to his feet. "You'll be sorry about this," he said, his warning like a growl coming from deep within him. "I'll find what I'm looking for, and you can't stand in my way."

He raced to his car and accelerated out of the driveway.

The siren grew louder. Flashing lights appeared on the road, and the deputy sheriff's car pulled into the barnyard. The deputy climbed from his vehicle. His gaze flicked from Luke to Becca who had reopened the kitchen door and hurried to join Luke.

Daniel stepped onto the porch and glared at Becca. "What is this?"

The deputy held up his hand. "Sir, stay where you are until I determine what's going on."

Daniel bristled.

Luke eased forward. "A man turned in to the barnyard and became belligerent when I asked him to leave."

Becca moved toward the sheriff. "The same man was here earlier today and demanded information and papers he thought I had received from the customer who died in the bakery explosion."

"Arnie Tuttle?"

Becca glanced at Luke. Evidently the sheriff's office had not yet determined Luke's father's real identity.

"Did Arnie give you anything?" the sheriff asked.

She shook her head. "Nothing except a Bible, but that is not what this man is searching for. The man entered Arnie's cabin and rummaged through his belongings. Arnie—" she used the alias "—gave me the key to his cabin, since he planned to be out of the area for a few days. I went there earlier today and surprised the man, who had broken in. He fled when I arrived."

The sheriff turned to Luke. "And you are?"

"A friend of Becca's." Luke provided his name.

She glanced at Daniel who, no doubt, wondered why Luke didn't reveal his relationship to the deceased victim.

The deputy pulled a notepad and pen from his pocket. "I'll need a description of the man and his vehicle."

Luke and Becca provided the information. The deputy

motioned Daniel forward. "Do you have anything to add to what they've provided?"

"I was inside and not aware of the problem."

The deputy called his office. "Put out a BOLO on a black sedan, tinted windows, Tennessee plates. The guy's white, bald, round face, approximately six-two, wearing a dark jacket, jeans and work boots."

Once he disconnected, he handed each of them his card. "Call me if he returns. I'll let you know if anything develops on our end."

"What about the autopsy?" Becca asked. "Yesterday, the sheriff mentioned one would be done."

"I'll check when I get back to the office. How can I contact you folks?"

Luke provided his cell number.

"I have a phone for business," Daniel shared the number. "Leave a message and I will return your call."

The deputy made note of the information.

"Has the cause of the explosion at the bakery been determined?" Luke asked.

"The fire marshal handles that side of the case. We should hear something soon. As I recall, someone at the scene mentioned smelling gasoline."

Becca had provided that detail, but she remained silent.

"The bakery ovens were fueled by propane. Could there have been a problem with the tank?" Daniel asked.

"Not likely unless someone tampered with it. Propane tanks are stable even under extreme conditions. They have an internal release valve that allows any built-up gases to escape. It's hard to make them blow." The deputy pursed his lips. "Of course, that doesn't mean it can't happen. Best advice is to wait until we hear from the fire marshal. You can call the sheriff's office and ask for that information in a day or two."

He nodded to Becca. "Especially since you were there, ma'am. Any idea if that man tonight had something to do with the explosion?"

"If he was looking for information, I doubt he would kill the man who had that information."

The deputy nodded. "That's a good point, which means if foul play is involved, there might be someone else who wanted to do harm."

"What about the owner of the bakery? Does he have any enemies?" Luke asked.

"Abraham Zook is well-thought-of in the area," Daniel inserted. "I cannot believe someone would seek to undermine his business."

The deputy looked at Becca. "This man tonight may have been coming after you, ma'am. Is there anything you're involved in?"

She raised her brow. "*Ack*, this is foolish talk. I work at the bakery. I have nothing to do with anyone with criminal intent."

The deputy raised his hand. "I wasn't implying that you did. The sheriff vouched for you, but I was just covering all the bases. There's talk that Tuttle may have been involved in something illegal."

Becca squared her shoulders. "Mr. Tuttle was a decent and honest man."

The deputy shrugged. "I'm just passing on what people are saying." He pointed to the barn and outbuildings. "Since I'm here, I'll look around and ensure the bald guy didn't leave evidence behind or anything that might harm you."

"I don't understand," Becca said.

"Ma'am, I don't have to tell you there was an explosion at a bakery where you worked. It seems plausible that someone other than the bald man may have triggered the explosion, but we can't rule anything out. If he wanted to destroy the bakery, he may want to bring harm to your farm as well."

Becca's heart lurched. She glanced at Daniel and then at the home where they had been raised, the home where Daniel and Katie planned to live after their marriage.

Gott, protect Daniel and our farm, she silently prayed. Her life had suddenly become so complicated.

The deputy pulled a flashlight from his vehicle and started toward the outbuildings. The flashing lights on his patrol car cut through the night and caught Luke and Daniel and herself in their glare.

If her father were still alive, he would have told the deputy to leave his farm, and he would have chastised Becca for bringing trouble into their peaceful life. She could see his narrowed gaze and the set of his jaw as he wagged his finger at her, just as he had done so many times.

Becca wanted to be strong and make her own way in life, but she seemed to be making mistakes no matter what she did.

Luke stepped closer and put his arm on her shoulder as if to offer support. Daniel noticed the action, and his expression hardened even more. "What have you done, Becca?" her brother said under his breath.

Which was what she was asking herself.

Had this happened because she wanted something more than living Amish? She feared it had.

SEVEN

The downstairs guest room was cramped and lacked electricity. Luke used the light on his phone to navigate the small area. The sheets were crisp and smelled like the outdoors. A quilt covered the bed, and he wondered if Becca had made the covering with her mother.

Daniel's and Becca's rooms were upstairs, which gave Luke freedom to move freely about the first floor of the house. He unlocked the kitchen door a number of times and checked outside. Sadie was there to greet him, and he felt sure she would bark if anyone came on to the property.

In the wee hours, he drifted to sleep and woke when the sound of pots and pans clanking together stirred him from his slumber. The house smelled of freshly baked biscuits when he entered the kitchen. No telling how long Becca had been working. The table was set, coffee brewed and a large skillet of ham and eggs warmed on the back of the stove.

"I was going to wake you soon," she said with a warm smile.

He glanced through the window to where Daniel worked with the horses in the paddock. "Evidently I'm the last to rise."

"I heard you in the night and glanced from my window to see you and Sadie searching the barnyard. I wondered if you got any sleep at all."

"A few hours."

She poured coffee into a large mug. "The sugar and cream are on the table."

He added both to his coffee and took a long swig of the hot brew. "Good coffee."

"Your father said the same thing on occasion."

He shook his head. "I kept thinking about what the people in town are saying about Andy Thomas being involved in something criminal."

"Would you believe gossips who have nothing better to do than spread lies?"

Luke nodded. "You've got a good point, Becca. Still, there could be truth in what is being said. I need to go to Waterbend to find the lawyer and talk to the people there. I tried to call McWhorter, but no one answered, and his voice mail was full. Someone must have information about what Andy was working on and why he left Tennessee and moved to a remote mountain cabin."

"I will go to Waterbend with you."

"What?"

"*Yah.* I have decided this is best. Your father was an important person in my life. He helped me deal with my own father's death, and he saw me for who I really am. I will not have lies spread about him. The truth will come out, Luke, and I want to make certain it does."

"I don't want you to go behind your brother's back."

"Let me make my own decisions. For some time now, I have yearned to see what life is like outside the Amish world. When my father was alive, I did as he directed. Some Amish youth have a period to explore other options, called *Rumspringa*. I did not do anything like my peers. Maybe that is why I have a need to be free of the Amish way for at least a few days. Daniel is taking some of his fall produce to the market in town this morning. Once he leaves, I will write a note and explain when I will return. If the bald man comes back, Daniel could stay with the Gingerichs until the authorities track down the assailant and determine what he wants."

"I… I can't stop you, Becca, and I wouldn't, anyway. As you mentioned, you have to live your own life."

"My aunt and uncle live in middle Tennessee. I checked a map last night and realized their farm is not too far from Waterbend. If I decide the fancy world is too much for me, I can stay with them."

"I would never keep you from something you feel is important, Becca, and I'm grateful that you're willing to help me uncover the truth about Andy. Having you at my side will be a huge help, so I'm the one who needs to thank you."

"It is *gut* we can work together. This is something your father would have wanted."

Andy Thomas might have, but he didn't think Daniel would be happy. Even so, Becca was her own woman, and Luke wouldn't stand in her way.

Although Becca was committed to helping Luke learn more about his father, she was also concerned about leaving her brother, especially with the bald man on the loose. Once Daniel left for town, she packed her Amish clothing and *kapp* in a tote and dressed instead as an *Englischer* in jeans and a blouse and sweater. Before leaving the house, she wrote a long note to Daniel explaining her actions before she and Luke took Sadie to the Gingerich house. They agreed to take care of the puppy, and Mr. Gingerich acted as if he understood Becca's need to make the trip with Luke. The kindly neighbor assured her they would invite Daniel to stay with them lest the bald-headed man return and try to do him harm.

"My eldest boy and I will help Daniel care for his livestock so he will not be alone on his farm in case the man returns. Do not worry."

Still, Becca was anxious as she and Luke left the Gingerich farm and rode down the mountain road. "Katie and her family will take *gut* care of Sadie, and hopefully they'll soothe my brother's upset when he returns from town."

She did not mention her concern for Daniel's safety. Nor did she mention her concern for her own safety or for Luke's well-being. The bald man had attacked her twice—two times too many. She breathed in a deep lungful of air and tried to focus on the trip and not the hateful man who thought she had the information he wanted.

Luke must have noticed her upset. "Are you sure you're comfortable going with me?"

"I am glad to help you." She offered him a weak smile and tried to appear upbeat. "How long will it take to get to Waterbend?"

He glanced at his GPS on his phone. "We'll stay on back roads. They're not as fast as the interstate, but we'll be away from the main highways and out of the public eye."

"You mean away from the bald man in case he's driving to Waterbend?"

Luke nodded. "We need to be careful." Glancing at his phone, he added, "The GPS says the trip should take a little over five hours. We'll stop for gas and something to eat."

"I packed a lunch in the smaller tote." She peered behind the seat to ensure the lunch basket was close by.

"That will save time. We'll head to the Institute, where

I lived, first. From there we can drive to Waterbend. It's about thirty minutes away, as I recall."

"How do you feel about going back to where you lived as a boy?"

"I haven't given it much thought, to be truthful. Maybe I don't want to think about it and just see what happens when we arrive on-site."

"Sometimes that is better. My mother said never to look at tomorrow until the day arrives."

Luke smiled. "Kind of like the *Englischer* saying of 'don't cross the bridge before you come to it.'"

"*Yah*, both mean the same thing. It is living in the present. My father said my mind was always elsewhere. He claimed I was like my mother in that regard."

"Was that a compliment?"

"In a way. I loved my mother dearly, and growing up, I always wanted to be like her."

"I'm sure she would be proud of you, Becca."

"Now you sound like your father. I often told him he should not be so affirming, but he said praise needed to be given when it was due. This is not something that the Amish believe in. They worry about a person becoming haughty and proud."

"Yet I can't see you letting the truth change you in any way."

She reached out and touched his hand. "Thank you, Luke."

They drove for a few hours and talked about their lives and what they hoped for in the future. Although they skirted any mention of the bald man, he remained ever on her mind. At noon, they pulled into a roadside park and ate the lunch Becca had prepared. Both of them were on edge and glanced at the nearby roadway whenever a vehicle drove by.

"Tennessee is beautiful," she admitted once they had finished eating.

"Haven't you been in the state before?"

"I visited my aunt and uncle a few times. My mother and I took the bus. It was an adventure, for sure." She glanced at his pickup truck. "Riding in your truck has been more enjoyable."

"On the drive to Mountainside, I was recalling too many things from my past and trying to decide what was true and what wasn't. Having a pretty lady to help pass the time makes everything much nicer."

Once they were on the road again, Becca began to wonder what they would find at the Institute. Things never were as they had been when a person went back, which was what her mother had told her when they had visited Becca's aunt and uncle. She had remembered those words and had mulled them over when she thought about leaving the Amish community.

As they drew closer to Luke's old home, she saw his eyes widen in wonder as he took in the scenery.

"Does anything look familiar?" She glanced at the thick foliage lining the road.

"Not really. My dad and I hiked in the hills around where we lived, but it's been so many years. I can't be sure of anything."

A sign pointed them toward the Tennessee Research Institute.

"We're almost there," he said.

She heard the anxiety in his voice and offered a silent prayer for Luke and what he would find.

"It should be just around the bend, according to my GPS." He made the turn and braked to a stop in front of a high fence topped with barbed wire. A padlocked gate barred them from driving on to the compound, and signs read Restricted Area, Do Not Enter.

A shiver ran along Becca's spine. This wasn't what she had expected, and the confusion on Luke's face said he didn't understand it, either.

"I don't know why the area is fenced off." Luke climbed from his truck and stood for a long time staring into the distance.

She followed his gaze and could make out a few red-brick buildings. "Is that the laboratory?"

He shook his head. "I believe those are administration buildings. The road in the distance leads to the housing area. This was the back gate, as I recall. Let's see if we can find the main entrance."

Becca glanced again at the warning signs and wondered if they would be welcome at any entrance. She didn't want to upset Luke, but it appeared the laboratory had shut down access not only to the research facility but also to the houses where Luke had lived.

Disappointment was evident in his expression, but she also saw the worry that washed across his face.

"I don't know what's going on, Becca. Things have changed here at the Institute, and not for the better."

They followed the narrow road along the periphery of the property until they came to what appeared to have been the main entrance at one time. The gate was secured with heavy chains and a series of padlocks. Just as at the back gate, signs on the fencing read Do Not Enter, Off-Limits, Private Property, Trespassers Will Be Apprehended.

"They are very explicit in not wanting anyone on the property." She blew out a stiff breath.

Luke parked, and they walked to the gate. In the distance, Becca could see the edge of a lake and the tip of the roof of a brick building near the water.

"A wooded area blocks our view of the residential area." Luke's voice filled with regret. "The homes were three stories with attic dormer windows, screened-in sun porches and rear patios that led to unattached garages."

He pointed to the hill beyond the Institute. "A fairly wide stream flowed along the foot of that hill and continued into town. I recall a path that meandered through the woods. It wasn't difficult terrain, but it felt like a real adventure when we'd hike there. In those days, the Institute wasn't fenced, and a footbridge crossed the stream, so it was easy to head into the hills."

"You and your dad?"

"Usually on Saturday afternoons. It was our 'guy time,' as he used to call it."

Luke wrapped his fingers through the latticed wrought iron on the gate. Becca reached up and touched his hand. "I know you had hoped to see your home."

"Foolishly I thought the current residents might let me take a peek inside." He pointed to the roadway. "Stay here. I'll jog along the path in case there's another entrance."

Hoping to catch sight of Luke's home, Becca stretched on tiptoe, then stuck her foot in the chain-link fence and climbed about three feet off the ground. Even from her lofty perch, she wasn't able to see any of the homes.

A twig snapped behind her. Startled, she jumped down, turned toward the sound and gulped. The barrel of a rifle was aimed directly at her. Her pulse galloped like a runaway mare.

"This is private property, lady."

The guy holding the weapon was big and muscular, with short-cropped hair and a snake tattoo on his forearm. He stood in front of a white SUV bearing a logo with the initials *TRI*, which undoubtedly stood for Tennessee Research Institute, superimposed on an outline of the state. The name tag on the left breast pocket of his navy blue polo read Hank.

Becca's heart pounded like a snare drum. She held up her hands to ensure the man knew she was unarmed. "I meant no harm and merely wanted a better view of the Institute."

"This is a restricted area."

He stepped closer, sending more warning signals off in her head. She recalled the bald guy who had gotten too close to her the day prior. Instinctively she stepped back and ended up flush against the fence. Unable to flee, she straightened her spine. "My mistake, but no harm done."

The guy's frown revealed his frustration and annoyance at her comment and made her even more unsettled.

Footsteps sounded. She glanced at the path and spied Luke as he hurried back to join her. He stopped short when he saw the rifle.

The guard narrowed his gaze as Luke moved closer to Becca. "Are you from around here?"

For a moment, Becca thought Luke might reveal his identity. Instead he shook his head and pointed back to the road.

"We were headed for Waterbend but must have taken a wrong turn. Either that or my GPS isn't working."

The guy stared at both of them for a long moment as if trying to determine the truthfulness of Luke's comment. Finally he motioned them toward their pickup.

"Head back to the main road. At the third intersection, take a right. Waterbend will be dead ahead."

Luke glanced again into the gated area and then at

the logo on the guy's SUV. "Is the Institute involved in scientific research?"

The guy pointed to the road. "You folks head to town and don't worry about what goes on here."

Becca touched Luke's arm. "We should go."

He glanced at the guard, then placed his hand on her back. Together they walked to his truck.

"What was that about?" Becca whispered when they were inside the vehicle.

"I don't have a clue." Luke turned the key in the ignition and slowly eased his pickup on to the main road.

"Hank made my skin crawl," Becca admitted.

"Not the welcoming committee I expected."

"You resemble your father. That's probably why Hank thought you looked familiar."

Becca tried to calm her racing heart once they were on the main road. Luke looked as concerned as she felt. Wanting to ensure they weren't being followed, she glanced back and gasped. "Luke, a white SUV is behind us."

"Surely he'll continue straight." Luke turned at the third intersection and accelerated along the well-paved roadway.

A few minutes later, he glanced at the rearview mirror. His face tightened.

A knot formed in her stomach when she realized the white security vehicle was still on their tail.

They had eluded the bald-headed man by leaving Mountainside, but now they seemed to be of interest to another man with a weapon.

Whatever Luke's dad had been involved in, she hoped Andy had been on the right side of the law. At the moment, she wasn't sure of anything.

EIGHT

Luke would be less worried about the obnoxious security guard who was following them if Becca wasn't in the car with him. The bald man had come after her in Mountainside, and now it seemed that Luke had driven her straight into another danger by deciding to visit his old home.

The high fencing topped with barbed wire and the many signs restricting entrance had been ominous enough. The bully of a guard made the situation even more unsettling. Knowing he was behind them added to Luke's concern.

"Coming to Waterbend may have been a mistake," he said when Becca glanced back again.

"The only way you can learn the truth about your dad is to return to where he lived and worked. Maybe the security guard planned to drive to town. His trip might have nothing to do with us."

Doubtful, but Luke didn't want to worry Becca unduly. He lifted his cell phone off the console and handed it to her.

"Do you know how to look up information on a phone?"

"*Yah*, Daniel keeps his in the barn for business purposes. I've used it many times."

"See what lodging's available in the area, although I

don't want Hank to know where we're staying, if that's possible."

"What's your access code?"

Luke provided the login. She tapped in the digits. "There's a hotel downtown and a motel called the Overnite Lodge off Rocky Road. It's a mile ahead."

"Do either of them look like secure accommodations?"

"There's a small B and B on the west end that appears more inviting."

"Tell me more about the one on Rocky Road."

"Hmm." She didn't sound encouraged. "From the website photos, it appears run-down."

"Perfect. We'll make the security guard think we're staying there."

"How are we going to do that?"

"Watch." He turned his truck on to Rocky Road and drove until the small motel appeared in the distance.

"Look back, Becca, and see if the guard is still following us."

"I don't see anyone coming around the corner." She touched Luke's arm. "No, wait. He's turning now."

Becca continued to glance back. "That's him. He's moving in this direction."

"There's the Overnite Lodge." Luke turned into the parking area and pulled to a stop.

Together they entered the small office. Luke glanced through a grimy window and saw the SUV park about twenty yards from the motel's driveway.

"He's waiting to see what we do," Luke said under his breath.

A man appeared from a back room. He had long hair, a scruffy mustache and beard, and thick bifocals that he peered over to, evidently, get a better look at his latest customers.

"You folks need a room?"

"Two rooms, preferably in the rear."

"Rooms 110 and 112 are available." The clerk tapped his computer screen. "Give me a name and a credit card and the rooms are yours."

"Paul Mason, and I'll pay in cash."

Luke pulled out his wallet and slipped the guy an extra twenty. "Let me know if anyone comes snooping around, and I'll be grateful. There's another twenty if you alert me when the guy parked near the driveway in the white SUV leaves the area."

The clerk peered through the dirty window and nodded. "Will do, Mr. Mason." He handed Luke the keys. "You folks enjoy your stay. If you need anything, call the front desk."

Luke glanced at the guy's name tag. "Thanks, Randy. I appreciate your help."

Once they were back in the truck, Luke turned to Becca.

"I doubt Hank will hang around very long."

"And we leave after he does?"

"That's exactly right. We can check out the B and B and see if they have a couple rooms. All the while, the guard thinks we're staying at the Overnite Lodge."

Becca nodded, although he could see the worry in her gaze. She wrung her hands and glanced at the white SUV as Luke backed the pickup away from the office.

They rounded the far side of the motel and parked in the rear. Luke grabbed his backpack and Becca's tote from his truck and opened the door to Room 110, which smelled of stale cigarette smoke and mildew. "I'm sorry. It's not pretty, but we won't be here long."

He held the door for her. Becca's eyes were wide when

she stepped inside. "Randy needs a better housekeeping service."

Luke placed their bags on the desk, then hurried to the window and eased back the curtain ever so slightly. As if on cue, the SUV appeared and pulled to a stop. Luke watched Hank talk to someone on his cell.

"I'm not sure who he's calling, but he must be reporting our whereabouts to his boss or coworker."

"Which doesn't make me feel any better."

"And makes me wonder who's interested in our location." He shook his head and sighed. "I'm sorry I brought you to Waterbend, Becca."

"You're not to blame. I'm an adult, and it was my decision to join you."

"Still, I led you into danger."

"I was in danger in Mountainside."

Luke was grateful for Becca's positive outlook. She was a levelheaded and determined woman who didn't need to be coddled. Yet she did need to be protected.

The SUV turned around and headed back to the front of the motel. Luke glanced through the window again and startled when the phone rang some minutes later. "I'll get it."

He lifted the receiver.

"It's the front desk, Mr. Mason. A guy stopped by, tattoo on his arm, TRI logo on his SUV. He wanted to know about you folks."

"What'd you tell him?"

"Only that you seemed like nice people. He asked me to call him when you checked out."

"He gave you his cell phone number?"

"Roger that."

"I'll take that number and give you a fifty if you tell

him we're heading to Ohio in the morning. How's that sound?"

Randy's voice bespoke his delight. "That sounds just fine. I'll write his number on a piece of paper and come round back to give it to you. If you folks are hungry, the trail through the woods at the rear of the motel ends up on a residential street. Turn left at the four-way stop, and you'll arrive at the center of town. You can find restaurants there."

"Thanks, Randy. We'll see you outside."

Luke hung up and shared what the clerk had said. He grabbed their bags and motioned Becca to the door. "You climb in the truck, and I'll pay the clerk. Randy earned his tip if Hank thinks we're driving to Ohio. That gives us time to visit a dear lady I'm sure you'll enjoy meeting."

A lady Luke hadn't seen for years, but he remembered the times she had taken him to her home to play with her grandson. If he could find her house on Sweetgum Street, he might be able to learn more about Andrew Thomas and what had changed at the Institute to make it a guarded enclave.

Becca was amazed at the way Luke had managed to provide a reprieve from the security guard whose motives for following them couldn't be *gut.*

"Shall I plug Sweetgum Street into your GPS?" she asked once left the motel.

Luke raised his brow. "You used the GPS on Daniel's cell?"

She smiled. "When we delivered farm items to customers who lived in outlying areas."

"I thought the Amish never used technology."

"Our district allows mobile devices for work purposes."

"Good to know." He pointed to his cell. "Try to find Sweetgum. I remember the street but not how to get there. A ten-year-old doesn't pay attention to directions."

Becca tapped in the street name. "It's on the other side of town, and not far from the B and B, which looks like a pleasant place to stay."

"Is there some way we can detour around the congested downtown area to get to Sweetgum?"

"Stay on this road until it dead ends, then turn left on to the outer loop that circles town. We'll continue on the loop for about five miles."

"That gives us enough time to see if the B and B has two rooms available for tonight."

"I'll call them now." Becca pulled up the B and B website and hit the Call for Reservations prompt.

A lady with a kind voice answered. "Waterbend Bed and Breakfast. This is Mrs. Edwards. How my I help you?"

"A friend and I are passing through town and wondered if you had two rooms for a couple nights. We would like to explore some of the beautiful outdoor trails around here if you have accommodations."

"Someone canceled their reservation not more than an hour ago, so I do have two rooms. Can I get your names and a credit card to hold the rooms?"

"Yes, of course." Becca covered the bottom of the phone. "She wants a credit card and the names we are registering under."

"What name did Andrew Thomas use?"

"Arnold Tuttle."

"Then I'll be Lucas Tuttle." He glanced at her. "What about you?"

"Your father called me Becky, so I'll use that name, and my mother's maiden name was Detweiler."

Becca provided their names to the receptionist and explained that they would pay in cash.

"If that's the case, you'll need to get here before six, otherwise I won't be able to hold the rooms."

"We'll be there well before then."

"Wonderful. I'll see you when you arrive."

Becca hung up and then shook her head. "I do not like to prevaricate, but I know it is necessary."

"I doubt we'll stay a long time with Miss Hattie. She's the sweet woman who helped my mother with housework. Although she'll probably encourage us to have a slice of her delicious peach pie."

"Sounds like she has some Amish blood."

"Her blood runs with hospitability and graciousness. It will be good to see her again. She took care of me when my parents went out."

"I'm sure she is a wonderful woman if your mother trusted her with your care."

Luke shrugged. "My mother enjoyed being the lady of the house more than she enjoyed being the mother of a ten-year-old boy."

The hint of sadness in his voice surprised Becca. "But you went willingly with your mother when she decided to leave your father."

"At that age, what could I do? I had to obey my mother."

"Then you agreed to be adopted by your mother's second husband."

"As a minor, my mother made the decision for me."

"How's your relationship now?"

He shrugged. "I rarely see her these days. As I mentioned, she's traveling in Italy."

Becca noticed a bitter edge to his tone. "I thought you and your mother were close."

"I love her, and I'm sure she loves me, but she's not the warm, fuzzy type of mom."

"I'm sorry, Luke."

"I'm not complaining, Becca. You deal with life the way it's handed to you. From what you've mentioned, your father wasn't the overtly demonstrative type, either."

"*Yah*, that is true. Some days I did not know if he wanted me around or if he would have preferred that I left home and struck out on my own."

"But you stayed with him."

"I was raised to be a dutiful child. Just as you said, I did what my father wanted, but only up to a certain point."

"Meaning?"

"He wanted me to marry an eligible Amish bachelor, but I refused to get involved with any of them."

"Because you were independent and wanted to make your own way in life."

"That is partially true. I also wanted to enter into marriage as a partner, an equal. This was not something the young Amish men I knew were willing to accept."

She glanced at his phone. "The turn on to Sweetgum will be on our right in three hundred feet."

"I see the road now." He activated the turn signal and eased on to the residential street. "Now to decide which house belongs to Miss Hattie Mayfield."

He tugged on his jaw. "I remember a pair of rocking chairs on her porch, a couple of large hydrangea bushes with purple flowers and a Welcome sign on the front door."

"The hydrangeas won't be in bloom this late in the fall, so we need to watch for rocking chairs and a Welcome sign."

"They could have been discarded by now and replaced with something else."

"Or Miss Hattie may have moved."

Becca studied the pretty homes that were modest but well cared for. Expansive lawns and overarching canopies of trees provided a warm ambience to the neighborhood.

She pointed to one of the houses. "There's a rocking chair and a Welcome sign, although it's faded and difficult to read."

His eyes widened. "I think we've found Miss Hattie's home." He peered at the small brick rambler. "There's a rear road that leads to the detached garage. Let's circle around and park in the back. It's doubtful the security guard would be driving through this older neighborhood, but I don't want anyone to connect me to Miss Hattie."

Just as Luke had mentioned, he parked in the rear, and then he and Becca circled the home on foot and walked to the front door.

"Let's hope she still lives here." He winked at Becca. "Also that she recognizes me. I've changed a bit since elementary school."

Becca tried to imagine a youthful Luke with his gold-streaked hair, big eyes and full cheeks. She envisioned the dimples that were noticeable when he smiled, which wasn't often enough, although at the present moment he wore an expectant grin.

Luke might be eager to connect with Miss Hattie, but Becca glanced around the attractive neighborhood and worried that things might not be as Luke remembered. Fifteen years was a long time. People changed, and not always for the better.

NINE

The eager anticipation Luke felt surprised him. He remembered Miss Hattie, but he'd never realized how important she had been in his life until this moment as he stood on her front porch. Becca's eyes were filled with understanding, as if she realized the emotions washing over him.

He pulled in a breath, glanced at the Welcome sign and knocked on the door. When no one answered, he rapped again and waited as footsteps sounded inside the house.

The door opened ever so slightly. Fearing it might close again, he took a step closer. "I'm here to see Miss Hattie Mayfield. My name is Luke Thomas."

No response came from the person, who must be peering out at him, then a gasp and a squeal of delight. The door opened, and Miss Hattie stood in the threshold. A smile spread over her face, and her eyes misted ever so slightly.

"Tell me it isn't so. Luke-boy, is that you, child?"

"Yes, ma'am. I came back to town and wanted to see you."

"You're all grown up into a handsome man. My, my, but your daddy would be so proud."

He hadn't expected her words to touch him so deeply

and to open up the longing he had carried for his father all those years.

"You make my heart happy just seeing you here. Come inside and let me give you a hug like when you were a little boy."

Luke didn't need to be coaxed. He stepped into the house and fell into her sweet embrace. Miss Hattie smelled of lilac toilet water, as she used to call it, and a floral-scented soap, just as she had when he was a boy. He remained for a long moment, basking in her love, before he realized Becca was still standing on the porch.

He pulled out of Hattie's arms and took Becca's hand, drawing her into the house. "This is a friend of mine, Becca Klein. She came with me and is helping me find information about my father."

"How nice to meet you, Becca. Welcome to my home, dear." She turned her warm gaze back to Luke.

"Your father left town about a year ago now, but let's visit awhile so we can catch up on what you've been doing all these years." She motioned them toward a room with overstuffed furniture and lace doilies that covered the tabletops and the backs of the chairs. A pretty afghan was draped over the arm of the couch, and a photograph of two young boys sat on an end table.

Luke stepped closer. "When did you take this picture?"

"Your daddy did, and he gave me a copy."

Luke held it out for Becca to see. "That's Miss Hattie's grandson, Nate."

"And you're next to him?" Becca asked.

He smiled. "I always had fun when I came to Miss Hattie's house. Nate lived down the street with his parents, and we'd run from here to Nate's house to get cookies at both spots."

"Nate would love to see you, Luke. He lives in Nashville, but he comes back often to see his parents. I'll find out if he's going to be home in the next few days."

"I'd enjoy seeing him for sure."

"I baked a pie this morning. The peaches were so plentiful this year. May I get you a slice along with a cup of coffee or a glass of lemonade?"

"I don't want to bother you, Miss Hattie." Luke held up his hand.

"Now, Luke-boy, you know that you could never bother Hattie. You're family, child." She touched her chest. "Just like my Nate, and that's the truth. As you boys used to say, 'Cross my heart.'"

Luke smiled, recalling how they often drew a small cross over their chests when they wanted to ensure Miss Hattie knew they were being truthful.

She motioned them forward. "Let's go into the kitchen, and we'll sit at the table. There's a view of my garden and some of the fall flowers—pansies and ornamental cabbage and kale that's in bloom."

"You always had a green thumb."

She held up her hand and chuckled. "Now, you know I've got a brown thumb, but my mama always said I had a way with plants."

Becca peered through the kitchen window. "Your garden is beautiful. Do you grow vegetables as well?"

"I used to, then I'd put them up and enjoy them through the winter." Hattie rubbed her back. "With my arthritis, I can't tend a garden like I used to. Now I buy my fresh produce from the grocery store, which is easier on my body."

She pointed them to the round table. "Sit down while I pour the lemonade and cut the pie."

"May I help?" Becca stepped toward the counter.

"That would be nice." Hattie pointed at the cupboard to the right of the sink. "You'll find glasses there. The ice is in the freezer, and the pitcher of lemonade is in the fridge. While you pour our drinks, I'll cut the pie."

Hattie's servings were large, and she shared stories from Luke's youth as they enjoyed the dessert. Luke was touched by the memories that gave him a clearer picture of his younger years. His mother rarely talked about when he was a little guy, but Hattie had stories about Luke and his family.

"I cried when I heard she left your father," Hattie shared. "Especially since that took you out of his life."

She leaned across the table and patted Luke's hand. "No father could love a son more than Mr. Thomas loved his Luke-boy."

"I... I didn't want to leave."

She nodded, knowingly. "Nothing you could have done when your mama wanted you to go with her. Mr. Thomas worked all those hours at the lab. He was a good provider, for certain. Your mama had everything she could ever need and then some." Hattie tsked and shook her head. "Such a shame that she gave it all away."

Luke had to agree. His whole world had been upended because his mother could not find happiness with the man she had married.

"We stopped at the Institute on our way into town. When did the fencing and all the Do Not Enter signs go up?"

The older woman thought for a moment. "The fence went up about three years ago, but the locked gates and warnings not to enter started a little over a year ago, around the time your father left Waterbend. The increased security came as a surprise to everyone. I was working for a nice lady who lived down from your parents' former home. I drove my car to the gate the day I was scheduled to work but couldn't get in. Nothing I could do to convince them I wouldn't cause no harm and that I just wanted to do my housework."

The look on Becca's face revealed she was as shocked as Luke was. "They wouldn't let you in?"

Hattie shook her head. "I asked them to call the lady I was supposed to work for. She met me at the gate and drove me to her house while I parked my car just outside the gate."

"Did anything look different inside the compound?"

"Nothing that I could tell except for more security vehicles. The guards drive white SUVs."

Becca touched Luke's arm. "Just like the one who followed us."

Luke explained about Hank following them to town. "That's why we parked in the rear of your property. I didn't want him driving by your house and seeing my truck."

"No one knows what's going on out there."

"You mentioned the house where my parents used to live. Did my father move out of our old home?"

Hattie patted Luke's hand. "Mr. Thomas moved to town not long after you and your mother left. I think the house was too big, with too many memories. I knew he missed you somethin' fierce, Luke. I could read it in his eyes and in the lack of joy on his face."

She turned to Becca. "Mr. Thomas was a delightful man who loved life and his family. Every time I saw him, he'd give me a big smile and inquire as to how I was. That man always had a compliment to share. Made me grateful to work for him and for Mrs. Thomas, but his joy ebbed after Luke left."

"You said he moved to town?" Luke repeated.

"Actually just outside town on Oak Lane. He bought

a small ranch house with some acreage so he could raise a few crops and have privacy. Although I'm not sure his supervisors approved of his move."

Luke didn't understand. "Why would that be a problem?"

"Your father was an important scientist at the Institute. They like to keep their employees where they can see them." She raised her brow. "At least that's what I've heard tell."

"From people who work there?"

"Not the scientists or the folks in management, but the people behind the scenes. Housekeeping, supply room clerks and facility maintenance. Those folks know how to stay in the background, but they hear things." She stared at Luke. "You know what I'm saying?"

"You're saying that management at the Institute controlled their employees. All this secrecy makes me wonder if some illegal activity was going on there, and if so, who was involved?"

Hattie raised her brow. "Meaning, was your father doing something illegal?"

"That's what I need to know."

"I cannot say for sure, but I know your father had a religious conversion of sorts after you and your mother left town. I don't remember your family going to church or your father being a prayerful man, but he got religion after you left. Divine Faith Church sits on Oak Lane inside the city limits. You can stop by and talk to Reverend Simpson. He'll tell you about the good your father did for the poor folks in the area, for single moms who fell on hard times, for kids who didn't have a dad. Mr. Thomas was always reaching out and offering help."

Her words felt like a stab to Luke's heart. He glanced

at Becca, and from the sorrow he saw in her eyes, he knew she understood his feelings.

Once again, Hattie patted his hand. "What I said hurt you, Luke, but I don't understand why. I never want to cause you to be upset."

"It's selfish on my part."

"You want to talk about it?"

Hattie could always read his heart.

"He helped so many in need, and that's wonderful, but he forgot about me, Hattie. He never tried to contact me by phone or mail or visit me."

"He didn't talk about it, but I know losing you cut his heart in two, and nothing would have pleased him more than to be reunited with his child. He never said, but I always suspected your mother was the reason."

"You mean she didn't want to see him again, so he stayed away from me as well. That doesn't make sense, Hattie. A lot of children from divorced families have relationships with both parents, even when the divorce is contentious."

"You are right, Luke, but your mother was strong-willed. I'm sure she insisted your father remain distant, even from you." She rubbed his hand. "Trust me when I tell you he loved you and wanted to be with you."

Luke pushed back from the table and carried his plate and glass to the sink, needing time to control his emotions. He didn't want to cry, but he felt a lump in his throat, and he knew his voice would be hoarse if he tried to speak. His reaction had taken him by surprise, and he was angry at himself for allowing his feelings to come to the surface. He had buried the pain of separation years ago, and he'd never expected it to surface again.

"The pie was delicious, Miss Hattie," he finally said. "Thank you for your kind hospitality today."

"I'm glad you and Becca stopped by to say hello, but I wish I could have provided more information about Mr. Thomas. He left town without telling anyone, but he kept his house, and a sweet lady is caring for the property. She lives in a one-story home just south of his ranch. Her name is Carol Rose. I'm not sure if you know her, Luke, but she knows all about you from Mr. Thomas. I feel sure she would open the house to you and allow you to look around."

"That would be wonderful, but we'll need directions."

"You mentioned the guard who was following you. Why don't I drive you to Mr. Thomas's house? It isn't far from here. I'll drop you off so there won't be a car sitting in the driveway to alert any security personnel in the vicinity. When you're finished looking around, call me, and I'll pick you up."

She carried her plate and Becca's to the sink, where Luke stood, peering out the window and trying to string together everything he'd learned today.

"Hattie had a *gut* idea about driving us," Becca prompted.

He nodded and swallowed hard. "We'd appreciate the help, but how will we get into the house?"

Miss Hattie picked up her cell. "I'll phone Carol and ask her to place the key under the doormat."

"Are you sure you feel up to driving us?"

"Of course, I do. I'll get my purse and make that call."

Hattie walked into the rear hallway, leaving Becca to rub her hand across Luke's shoulders. "Are you okay?"

He sighed. "Just a little unsettled by the feelings that have surfaced. I never expected visiting my old hometown would cause so many memories to bubble up anew."

"You've held in your emotions for a lot of years.

They're starting to surface, which is *gut*, but that also adds to your confusion."

"I thought I knew everything about the man who was my father. Now I'm learning things I never would have imagined."

"All that buried hurt needs to heal, Luke. If it remains buried, it continues to fester, and that woundedness grows like gangrene. *Yah*, it hurts as it bubbles up, but once it is out in the open, then the wound can knit together from the inside."

"There will always be a scar, Becca."

She smiled sweetly, and her hand had a soothing touch, not like a mother's touch, but as a friend who understood his upset.

"We all have scars, Luke, but they are signs of our growth and our ability to overcome the pain from our past."

He turned to face her, and without forethought, he wrapped his arm around her and hugged her. "Thank you, Becca, for being with me and for helping me."

Hattie's footsteps in the hallway alerted them to her return. Becca took a step back, not wanting to embarrass Luke or to send the wrong signal to the sweet older lady.

"I talked to Carol. Here's her cell number and mine as well." Hattie handed Luke a small card with both phone numbers. "Carol's heading to Mr. Thomas's house now and will leave the key under the mat. Return it there when you're finished looking around. Or she mentioned that if you wanted to stay at the house, she could put sheets on the beds in the two guest rooms, and you could keep the key for as long as you needed a place to stay."

"We've already made arrangements to stay at the Waterbend B and B," Luke said.

"Mrs. Edwards is the owner. She's a lovely woman. I've

cleaned for her a few times when she was short-staffed. I'm sure you'll enjoy your stay."

Hattie reached for her handbag and keys. "Carol asked if you knew when your father would return to town."

"Oh, Hattie, I never told you."

She pursed her lips. "Tell me what, Luke-boy?"

"We were so busy learning information about Mr. Thomas that we—" Becca stared at Luke.

He didn't want to be the bearer of bad news, but Hattie needed to know.

"For the last year, Mr. Thomas lived in a rural part of the North Georgia mountains," Becca explained. "I worked at a bakery there, and he would always stop in for doughnuts on Tuesday when I baked the raspberry-filled variety."

Hattie smiled weakly. "His favorite."

Becca nodded. "That's what he always said. On his last visit…" She bit her lip and reached for Luke's hand. He wasn't sure if she was trying to offer him support or if she needed support as well.

"Becca called me a few hours later," he interjected. "I drove to her mountain community the next day. That's when Becca and I met."

"I… I don't understand," Hattie admitted.

Revealing what had happened was difficult. He glanced into sweet Miss Hattie's eyes just as the lump returned to his throat.

"There was an explosion in the bakery. Becca had gone outside, thankfully, but—"

She took up where he left off. "Mr. Thomas was still inside. He didn't survive the explosion, and a fire consumed the entire bakery."

"Oh, no!" Hattie stumbled back and lowered herself into a nearby chair.

Luke stepped to her side. "I... I should have told you when we first arrived."

"It wouldn't have changed my hurt or my anger."

"Anger?" He'd never known Miss Hattie to be angry about anything.

"The Institute, Luke. Something bad is happening there, and it involves your father. For whatever reason, they were trying to do him harm."

"But you said he wasn't working on anything illegal."

"Your father must have been trying to bring the crime to light, but they came after him, and they found him and killed him. I'm sure of it."

She grabbed Luke's hand. "You have to find out what's going on, Luke, to clear your father's name and to end their wrongdoing."

"I don't know if I can, Hattie."

"I will pray, and God will provide."

Luke wanted to learn the truth about his father. The Institute was trying to cover up something, and he needed to find out what.

Becca slipped into the back seat of Miss Hattie's car after Luke parked his pickup in her garage.

"I'll drive you to your father's house and drop you off," the older woman said. "Call me when you're ready to be picked up."

Becca liked seeing the pretty downtown area. Waterbend was small but well maintained. Luke pointed out a few landmarks he remembered from his youth, and Hattie continued to share a bit about how the area had grown.

"This is Oak Lane," she announced as she turned on to a two-lane road that headed into the country. They hadn't gone far when she indicated a ranch house in the distance. "That's Mr. Thomas's home."

The house had a large picture window in the front, and although the drapes were drawn, Becca knew the living area must be bright and cheery. A porch rimmed the front of the home, and shrubs circled the periphery of the house. The door and shutters were painted white and stood out against the redbrick. A wrought iron fence edged the porch, and two rocking chairs provided an inviting welcome.

"Where does Ms. Rose live?" Luke asked after staring for a moment at the house.

"Her home is on the opposite side of the road. See the small clapboard one-story?"

Luke nodded, and Becca smiled at the manicured lawn and sculptured bushes. A row of winter pansies rimmed her porch. "Ms. Rose appears to be a gifted gardener like you, Hattie."

The sweet woman chuckled. "We're of one heart when it comes to plants and flowers." She pointed back to Luke's dad's place. "Carol keeps Mr. Thomas's yard impeccable. Look at those hostas and azaleas. Even her geraniums are flourishing, and it's well into the fall."

Becca agreed that Andy's yard was well maintained. "Is there any chance she might stop by to say hello?".

"Carol's a private person, so I'm not sure, but I know you would enjoy meeting her."

"I hope I can express my thanks for the care she's provided to my dad's house and surrounding grounds, but if I don't get to see her, be sure to let her know my gratitude."

Once again, Luke had referred to Andy as his dad. Progress was being made even if Luke didn't recognize the change.

Miss Hattie pulled in the drive and waited until they exited her car. With a wide smile and a wave, she backed on to the street and headed to town.

Luke stood staring at the house.

"It's a lovely home," Becca reassured him.

He pointed her toward the front door. "Let's find the key and go inside."

The interior of the home was neat and tidy. They stepped into a small foyer that led to a relatively large main living area. Even with the drapes drawn, the room was bathed in light. Prints of wildlife hung on the walls— a giant eagle soared over a mountain, a pair of cardinals pecked at a tree's bough laden with berries, a mama blue jay hovered over her nest.

"These look like original watercolors." Luke studied the signed and numbered prints.

"They're beautiful." Becca turned to the fireplace and was surprised to see a large carved cross hanging over the mantel, which underscored Hattie's mention of Andy's deep faith.

Bookshelves edged the room, and a collection of aged Bibles was arranged on one shelf. As much as Becca wanted to pull them out and carefully gaze at the pages, she knew they needed to stay with the collection of old tomes and classics that Luke's father must have enjoyed not only reading but also collecting. She ran her finger over the leather bindings of a number of her favorites— *A Tale of Two Cities*, *Robinson Crusoe* and *Moby Dick*, among others.

"Your father enjoyed classical literature." She eyed Luke. He seemed interested in the titles as well.

Her gaze moved again to the mantel. She picked up the five-by-seven snapshot of a boy who couldn't have been more than six or seven, with wide eyes, an engaging smile and shaggy blond hair. "That has to be you."

Luke turned to stare at the photo. A flash of recognition brightened his face.

She pointed to a picture of an attractive woman with a child who was undoubtedly Luke. The woman stood to the side of the child with her hands clasped in front of her as if to ensure the child who glanced up at her wouldn't take her hand. The woman had an aloof air that was noticeable even in the photo. "This is you with your mother, *yah*?"

"Yah," Luke replied, using her Amish phrase. "As I recall, that was my first day of school, and I didn't want to go. Hattie suggested taking the photo before she walked with me to the bus stop. Mother was less than thrilled to have her picture taken—not that she disliked posing for a photograph, but she rarely wanted to have her picture taken with me."

Becca found it hard to imagine a mother who would openly reject a photo with her child.

"A case study in a psychology class I had in college made me wonder if she didn't want to admit her age. Having a son could have added years to what she considered her youthful appearance."

"Yet she took you with her when she left your father."

"Ironic, isn't it? My mother's actions have never been easy to understand."

Hearing the sadness in Luke's voice, she pointed to a trifold frame on a side table. "Look at you here. Were you hiking with your dad?"

He drew nearer and smiled. "We both loved forging through the forest." He pointed to a larger photo on a desk in the corner of the room. Luke held a fishing pole in one hand and a good-size trout he had snagged in his other. "I was so proud of myself that day. Dad called me an angler extraordinaire."

He pulled open the top desk drawer and inhaled sharply.

"What is it?" Becca stepped closer and placed her hand on Luke's, hoping to provide solace.

"A paperweight I made out of clay. It was a Father's Day gift the year before we left."

"Your father treasured it, no doubt, to keep it all these years."

"He said he did when I gave it to him." Luke picked it up and then stared at the folded paper under the clay.

"Did you find something else?" Becca followed his gaze.

Luke unfolded the paper. "It's the note I wrote to him before Mother and I left the house. She had surprised me with the news about leaving when I came home from school that day. I didn't want to go, as I mentioned to you earlier, so I hastily scribbled this note and placed it under his paperweight, hoping he would see it there."

He stared at the childish script as Becca read it aloud. "'Mom's making me go with her. I don't want to leave you.'"

She squeezed his hand. "Oh, Luke, I'm so sorry for all the pain you experienced as a young child."

He refolded the paper and returned it to the drawer and placed the clay paperweight over it. Then he pushed the drawer closed.

She wrapped her arm around his shoulder and rested her head on his arm. More than anything, she wanted Luke to know how much his dad had loved him.

"I… I never thought coming back to town would be so hard."

"As I've told you before, Luke, your father loved you."

He gazed into her eyes. The sorrow that covered his face nearly broke her heart. "All I wanted as a child was to see my dad again, but he disappeared from my life that day, which broke my heart."

TEN

Luke had to pull himself together. He was showing his vulnerability, and he had worked for so long to ensure he didn't dwell on the past, but coming back to town had brought so many memories to mind. "I'm learning who my father was," he told Becca. "Although I can't forgive him for not coming to find me."

"I am sure your father had a reason that will make sense if and when it comes to light."

He hugged Becca, then stepped from her arms. She was an Amish woman who did not need to be pulled into his confusion.

"Maybe there's something else in the desk." He opened the two side drawers and rustled through the pens and notebooks. "Nothing seems of interest here."

"What about the bottom drawer?"

The drawer contained a number of scientific magazines and a farming publication. He pulled them out and fanned the pages, then stopped to study one of the articles.

"'Tennessee Research Institute and their Agricultural Department.'" He turned the page so Becca could read the title. "I didn't know the Institute was involved in agriculture."

He settled onto the couch and glanced over the article. "It appears the Institute was close to announcing a breakthrough in crop production."

Becca narrowed her brow. "I thought they were involved in medical research."

"Not necessarily, but agriculture seems a bit out of step." He looked at the cover. "This edition is a little over a year old."

"Published not long before your father left the Institute and moved to Georgia."

"I wonder if that's significant," Luke mused.

"Does it mention the scientists involved in the project?"

Pulling the magazine closer, he tapped a picture and held it up for Becca. "Look at that photo."

She leaned closer. "It's Andy, clean shaven, with short hair."

"Evidently he had something to do with the research."

"Yet he left soon after the magazine was published."

Luke continued to read. "It doesn't mention the scientists' names who worked on the project, but it does say a wealthy philanthropist was interested in marketing the product once it was ready for distribution."

"Who's the philanthropist?"

Luke glanced again at the article. "It doesn't provide a name."

He thumbed through the next magazine and found a small piece about a new product developed at a Tennessee firm that would impact farming, with more information to follow.

Glancing at the first few paragraphs in a third article, he said, "This story in *Farming Life* questions the ethical integrity of the remote and secretive research lab working on something new for crop production."

"Does it say what's questionable about the lab?"

Luke shrugged. "Let me read a bit more." He glanced

at the bottom of the page and then turned to the end of the article near the back of the magazine. "Evidently there's some dispute about who has legal rights to a new product."

Becca glanced at the cover. "That's the farm magazine?"

Luke nodded. "The story doesn't mention the Institute, but it talks about a gated rural Tennessee laboratory where secrecy is important." He glanced up at her. "This article was published right before my father left Waterbend."

He handed her the magazine. "See what you think." As she reached for the publication, a slip of paper fell to the floor.

Luke picked it up. The name Rex was written on the paper along with a phone number.

"I wonder who Rex is?"

Becca glanced at the article and tapped the page. "The writer's name is Rex, and he's mentioned in the concluding paragraph of the piece. 'Rex Bryant is a freelance investigative journalist who regularly reports on farming, soil pollution and the harmful products ruining crop production. Bryant lives in the Nashville area and writes frequently for farm publications.'"

Luke stared at the slip of paper with the phone number.

"Looks like I need to call Rex and see why his name and number, as well as the article he wrote, were in my father's desk."

The doorbell rang, and Becca watched Luke pull the curtain back a tiny bit to peer outside. "It's an older woman. My guess is it's Carol Rose."

A woman with gray-blond hair and big blue eyes greeted him when he opened the door. "You're Luke. I could recognize you anywhere, the way you look like

Mr. Thomas. He talked about what a fine young man you were."

"Come inside, please." Luke motioned the kindly neighbor into the foyer. He introduced Becca and checked the street to make certain a security vehicle wasn't nearby as the women chatted.

"You took care of my father's house while he was gone," Luke said once he was assured the street was clear.

"I hope you found everything in good order. Your father managed the house when he was here, but he asked me to look after things when he left town."

"Did he mention why he was leaving?"

"Only that he needed to protect something he was working on."

"The project he developed at the Institute?"

"I think so, although what I know is secondhand information." She glanced at the door Luke had closed. "I take care of folks who need a little help. Two ladies have dementia and their husbands have me stay with their wives when they go away on trips."

"That is a ministry as well as a job," Becca said.

Carol's eyes glowed, and she seemed pleased by the comment. "That's how I feel. I like to help folks, especially when they're in need. That's why I agreed to care for Mr. Thomas's house."

She paused for a moment, and Luke waited, sensing she had more to add. "There is a lovely woman who works in housekeeping at the Institute and needs someone to watch her mom when she's at work each Tuesday and Thursday."

Luke glanced at Becca, who was smiling. "Often we would chat when she came home from work," Carol continued. "That's how I learned about Mr. Thomas's upset with the Institute."

Luke's attention piqued. "In what way, Carol?"

"He was the lead scientist working a big project. A man named Joseph Morris assisted him in the lab."

"I remember a kindly man named Mr. Morris. He came to the house a few times to meet with my dad. He loved baseball and brought me a signed photograph of Tom Glavine. He was an Atlanta Braves favorite of mine."

"Joe's a baseball fan for sure." Carol nodded in agreement. "My housekeeping friend said Mr. Morris seemed upset at work, and she overheard him talking to another employee about the Institute trying to take over Mr. Thomas's project. The fence was up at that time, but the gates were kept open in the daytime. Soon after that, the gates were padlocked and the Do Not Enter signs appeared. Your father said he would be leaving town in a few weeks, then two days later, I found a note in my mailbox along with his house key, saying he would be gone for a number of months."

She glanced at Becca. "Mr. Thomas was generous almost to a fault. Talk to anyone at his church, and they'll say the same."

Becca stepped closer to Luke. "That's the Andy Thomas I knew. A good man to the core."

"You've got that right. He arranged a monthly deposit in my bank account as a thank-you for watching his house and property. He didn't need to pay me. I would have helped him without the money, but he wanted to ensure I was reimbursed for my effort."

Luke looked down at the magazines still in his hand. "Do you know anything about the big project the Institute was ready to release?"

"That was right before your father left. I thought it was your father's work that they were trying to claim belonged to the Institute. Joe Morris might have more information."

"He's still in Waterbend?"

"He has a room at the senior rehab center in Hartwell. It's the next town north of here."

"He became infirm?"

"An auto accident. He was leaving the lab. There was a storm, and the road was slippery. Mr. Morris was trying to salvage some of the data after your dad left town. He claimed a truck ran him off the road and into a ditch, although the security guards said no other vehicle was in the area. According to them, video surveillance cameras confirmed their statements."

Carol raised her hand. "Of course, you never heard any of this from me, right?"

"We would never involve you in whatever is going on," Luke said. "I greatly appreciate all you've done for my father and for what you've shared with us today."

"You're right." She leaned closer and lowered her voice. "Something *is* going on at the Institute, and it affected Mr. Thomas. That's why he left town. I pray he's safe, wherever he is."

Luke could feel Becca's support when she took his hand. He couldn't tell Carol about his father's tragic death at the moment, but he would when he had more time. Something ominous was afoot, and Luke needed to uncover the truth.

Becca and Luke checked the rest of Andy's house after Carol left but found nothing more of interest. They called Miss Hattie, and she arrived soon thereafter and drove them back to her place.

"Stop by tomorrow for lunch," she insisted as they

climbed into Luke's pickup. "I'll make some of the foods you enjoyed as a child."

"We'll stop by, but don't go to any trouble."

Knowing they would see Miss Hattie the next day comforted Becca, as she'd been drawn to the sweet older lady. "The people in this town are so very nice," she told Luke as they drove to their lodging.

"Everyone has had good things to say about my father, which is encouraging."

"I'm glad you came here so you could see him in a better light."

"If only we knew more about my father's project. I'll call Rex once we check into our rooms. Perhaps he can provide more information about the Institute and what my father was working on."

"What about the lawyer?"

"McWhorter? I'll call him again."

Luke parked his truck on the narrow road behind the B and B. He grabbed their bags and ushered Becca through a rear door. Mrs. Edwards, the owner, according to her name tag and Miss Hattie's comment, appeared surprised to see them arrive through the back access. Luke mentioned wanting to park in the shaded area behind the lodge. The woman accepted his explanation and was gracious and cheerful as she checked them into their rooms.

"Becky's room is on the first floor and faces the patio and flower gardens. If weather permits, breakfast will be served there in the morning and runs from seven until nine thirty. I'll have freshly baked cookies in the parlor this evening, along with tea and coffee before you retire."

"That sounds lovely." Becca smiled.

The owner turned to Luke. "I've got you on the second floor at the top of the grand staircase, Lucas."

Becca hated that they'd registered under aliases, but they needed to ensure the security guard did not learn of their whereabouts.

"There's a nice restaurant within walking distance if you're interested in dinner this evening. The food is good, as is the service." Mrs. Edwards pointed to the road in front of the lodging. "Go to the end of the next block, and turn right toward the center of town. The Country Chef will be on the corner."

After thanking the owner, they went to their individual rooms. Soon thereafter, Luke knocked on Becca's door. She invited him into the sitting area separate from the bedroom. "The accommodations are lovely, Luke."

"I'm glad you found this place," he agreed. "I called Rex, but no one answered, so I left a message saying I wanted to talk to him about the Institute and the article he wrote in *Farming Life*."

"And if he does not return your call?"

"I'll try again later. I also phoned the lawyer, but his voice mail is still full. Tomorrow morning, I would like to visit the senior rehab center in Hartwell and talk to Mr. Morris before we meet Miss Hattie for lunch."

"Speaking of food, we should probably head to dinner."

Luke glanced at his watch. "The night air will be cool. You might want to wear a jacket to the restaurant."

Becca pulled a windbreaker from her tote. Luke helped her slip it on before they left her room. "I'm not used to wearing *Englischer* clothing."

"You look lovely either way."

Just as the owner had said, the restaurant was close by, and their dinner was delicious. "If I lived here," Luke admitted once they had finished eating, "I'd make it a point to enjoy the Country Chef's cooking on a regular basis."

"Even his dessert was perfect."

"You said my dad enjoyed raspberry-filled doughnuts?"

Becca nodded. "He had a sweet tooth for sure, and the jelly-filled doughnuts were his favorites. I baked them on Tuesdays, which is the reason he always stopped by on that day. Usually he would take a dozen cookies and some pastries home as well. He was my best customer."

"What happens when you go back to Mountainside, Becca, now that the bakery is gone?"

"The Zook family owned the shop. Whether they will rebuild, I do not know."

"Have you ever thought of owning your own bakery?"

She stared at him across the table. "This would be difficult, since I have no collateral. As a dutiful Amish daughter, I gave a portion of my earnings to my father when he was alive and then to my brother after *Datt*'s death. A farm has expenses, and I needed to contribute as well."

"How soon will Daniel and Katie wed?"

"It will not be long from now. Almost two months. The time will pass quickly, plus there is much to do to prepare for their marriage."

"The ceremony will take place at Katie's parents' home?"

"*Yah*, but I will help, and then I must ready my father's house for her."

"Yet you won't be staying there."

"I do not know what I will do. The woman who runs the produce market located near the bakery had a room for rent in her home. I could have managed there, but now that the bakery is gone—"

Luke took her hand. "Can I help you?"

"Oh, Luke, you are generous like your father. I will find my own way."

"I can take you back to Mountainside whenever you want, Becca. You didn't sign up for all this mystery when you agreed to come with me."

"I want to stay until you find out what's going on. Forgive me if I seemed ungrateful."

"It's not that, but I'm worried about your safety, especially if Hank appears again."

"And when I go home, the bald-headed man might still be there."

"If Daniel stays at Katie's house and you are nowhere to be found, I have a feeling he will leave town."

That was Becca's hope as well.

He paid the bill, and they walked back to their lodging. Night had fallen, and Becca was aware of every shadowed alcove where a person could hide.

A car approached on the street. Luke ushered her toward the entrance to one of the stores that angled away from the street and let out a sigh of relief when the car passed.

"I'm worried," she said when they returned to the sidewalk. "Having food delivered to the B and B might have been a safer option."

"We'll be there soon, then we can relax."

A sign in the lobby said guests would need to use their keys to enter the B and B after 9:00 p.m., but when Luke walked Becca to her room, they both saw the large windows in the living area, the back door where they had gained access earlier and the side panels on the front door that could easily be broken.

"Lock your door and check that the windows are secure." Luke's voice was low. "You can dial my room number on the landline in your room if you're worried about anything."

"I'll be fine," she assured him. "What time do you want to have breakfast?"

"How 'bout eight thirty?"

"That sounds perfect. Call me in the morning, and I'll meet you on the patio."

She gave him a gentle hug. "Good night, Luke. *Slaap wel.*"

He raised his brow. "Do you mind translating?"

She laughed softly and looked down the hallway to ensure she hadn't disturbed any of the other guests.

"I said sleep well."

He smiled, then reached out and ran his hand along her cheek. "Just as I told you before, Becca, call me if you are concerned about anything."

"And you can call me as well."

She slipped into the room and closed the door. The lock dropped into place. She listened for his departing footfalls. Hearing nothing, she realized he was still in the hallway. She thought of his green eyes and angular face and how safe he made her feel. It was a *gut* feeling that warmed her heart.

Luke was concerned about Becca's safety. He stood for a long moment in the hallway outside her room, then pulled in a deep breath and thought of the Lord. He had stopped praying long ago, believing God didn't listen to a little boy brokenhearted about his father suddenly stripped from his life. But Becca had faith, and he wondered if God would listen to his prayer for her.

"I fear Becca could be in danger tonight," Luke whispered. "Please, Lord, keep her safe."

He headed into the main part of the expansive lodging. After ensuring the various exits were locked, he checked the windows and opened a number of closets and cubby-holes to confirm no one was there hiding.

At long last, he climbed the stairs to the second floor and peered from the window in his room to the patio below. The outdoor lighting that had been on earlier was now off, probably on a timer, casting the patio in darkness. The wind blew, stirring the trees and causing shadows to dance across the flagstones.

Tomorrow Luke would take Becca home. She needed to be safely back in her Amish environment, but the thought of saying goodbye to her tugged at his heart.

Again, he called out to the Lord. "If You can hear me, help me straighten out my life. Even more than that, keep Becca safe. I could never forgive myself if something happened to her."

ELEVEN

Becca checked the windows as Luke had suggested and found them locked. She liked Luke. In fact, she liked him more than she wanted to admit. He had a *gut* heart and was concerned about others, just as his father had been. But something more appealed to Becca.

When he had touched her cheek before saying good night, a current had traveled through her that made her want to lean closer and inhale his scent—a mix of clean soap and aftershave.

It had been somewhat brazen of her to hug Luke, but she had done so without forethought, and then once she was in his arms, she didn't want to step away. The same electric current had been like a magnet *both* times his hand had touched her cheek. In the midst of her confusion, she had chosen the coward's way and retreated into her room.

Now she wished she had remained in the living area so they could have talked longer. Yet, he was tired and no doubt needed sleep. She did, too, but she wondered if she could unwind enough to allow sleep to overtake her. Right now, all she could think about was Luke and his understanding gaze, full lips, warm smile, broad shoulders, strong arms—

"Stop!" she said aloud.

She needed to turn her thoughts to something else. Daniel came to mind.

Tomorrow she would use Luke's cell phone to call Daniel's business line and leave a message so he would know she was all right. She owed him that. Daniel was a wonderful brother, and he had a lot on his mind with the farm and his upcoming marriage. He didn't need to worry about his wayward sister as well.

Concern for him swept over her, and she knew she had to make the call tonight. She dialed Luke's room number on the room phone to ask him to meet her in the lobby with his cell and then sighed with frustration when the landline connection failed to work. Surely Luke wasn't asleep yet. She grabbed her key, left her room and walked quietly into the main lobby. A small lamp was on in the corner. As she headed to the grand stairway, something outside the large picture window caught her eye. She stopped and stared, then pulled in a deep breath as a man peered through the glass. Not just any man, but Hank, the security guard. How had he tracked them to the B and B?

She backed against the wall, grateful for the darkness in her area of the room, and watched as he tried the rear door. Her heart nearly stopped, knowing if the lock wasn't engaged, he would enter the lobby within seconds.

"Please, *Gott*," she said under her breath.

She gripped her hands and tried to calm her pounding heart, fearing Hank could hear her even through the glass. Again, he peered inside and rattled the doorknob, over and over again.

Taking something out of his pocket, he leaned down and attempted to pick the lock. Her heart nearly stopped.

If she had a cell phone, she would have called 911, but she didn't, and the house phone was across the room, near the lit lamp—where Hank would see her.

He tried the knob, then, to her relief, he returned whatever instrument he had used to his pocket, tugged on the doorknob once again and then continued on along the back alleyway. Becca ran to the stairs and took them two at a time. At the landing, she searched for Luke's room, then tapped on his door.

It flew open. He was still dressed, and his expression was one of concern. "Something happened?"

"Hank. He tried to enter the B and B through the rear door."

Luke pulled her into his arms as he reached for his cell and called 911.

"Someone attempted a break-in at the rear door of the Waterbend B and B." He provided the address. "No one gained access, but there's a guy in the area." He gave a description of Hank and his SUV.

"He works for the Institute."

Becca leaned closer and heard the dispatcher's reply. "He has jurisdiction in town as well as at the research facility."

Luke bristled. "What does that mean?"

"Sir, that means he was probably checking the door instead of trying to break in."

Becca gasped at the operator's reply. The Institute had more power than either she or Luke had realized. They controlled not only the research lab where Andy had worked but also had some influence in town.

"Hank notified us earlier about two people trying to gain access to the research facility," the 911 operator continued. "He followed them to town and is trying to track them down."

"But he's a security guard." Luke rubbed his hand over Becca's trembling shoulder.

"Yes, sir. Hank used to work for the sheriff's department. He's considered one of our team."

"Your team of law enforcement?"

"That's correct. He'll make certain anyone causing problems is not allowed access to the laboratory or to any of the local businesses, you can be assured of that."

Luke disconnected and pulled Becca tighter into his arms. "We'll leave here in the morning. It's too dangerous now with Hank prowling around outside."

He motioned Becca toward the small seating area at the top of the stairs. From there, they could peer down at the rear door and into the patio beyond. "We'll hunker down here tonight. I'll keep watch to make certain Hank doesn't enter the B and B."

"I had planned to use your cell to call Daniel and leave a message on his phone, but I'm too upset and afraid he might hear the anxiety in my voice."

"You can call him tomorrow."

She nodded and settled into an overstuffed chair. Luke ran down the stairway and checked the back door before he disappeared along the hallway where her room was located. He returned within a few minutes and climbed the stairs.

"The doors are secure. No one appeared outside either in the front, the rear or on the side patios, but I don't want to leave now and chance running into Hank in the dark. Breakfast is served at seven, which means the owner or one of her staff should arrive sometime before that to begin preparing the morning meal. That's when we'll check out."

Becca's heart continued to pound as she thought again of Hank trying to pick the lock on the rear door.

"First," Luke added, "we'll stop at Miss Hattie's and tell her we're leaving town."

Becca looked into Luke's troubled gaze. The hallway was lit by two lamps that sat on a credenza at the rear of the landing. Even in the muted light, she could see his upset and understood his desire to see Miss Hattie one more time.

"She would be devastated if you left town without saying goodbye, Luke."

"Thanks for understanding."

His face relaxed, and she read gratitude in his gaze. Tired from all that had happened, Becca rested her head against the back of the chair and closed her eyes. The tension she had felt earlier eased. She was safe with Luke and knew he would protect her.

Luke heard Becca sigh before her breathing shallowed into what seemed like a light slumber. He hated the mistakes he had made, one after another. Inviting her to join him on his trip to Waterbend had been his first error, much as he liked having her with him. His second mistake had been to stop at the Institute. Having Hank on their tail compounded all their problems.

Luke peered at Becca's closed eyes and sweet face. She was beautiful, but in a pure way that bespoke an inner serenity as well as an outer attractiveness that had gotten his attention the day they met. In a short period of time, he had realized what really made her so alluring—she was considerate of others and focused on their needs instead of her own.

He sat in a straight-back chair close to the stairwell and continued to glance through the large window and peer into the darkness outside. He cocked his ear and listened for any sounds that weren't common to the night.

Time passed slowly, but he remained vigilant, and after a few hours had gone by, he headed downstairs again and checked the doors to make certain they were locked. Glancing out the windows, he could see the wind blowing through the trees. Shadows played over the patio and garden area, giving him cause for concern. Hank could be hiding anywhere in the darkness.

With the first light of dawn, the click of high heels sounded from below as the owner headed to the registration desk and checked her computer.

A second woman wearing an apron over her slacks and sweater asked something about breakfast.

Luke backtracked to the chair where Becca slept. He touched her arm and called her name ever so quietly. She opened her eyes and started to straighten herself. He put his finger to his lips and then pointed to the first floor. She rubbed a hand over her cheeks and followed his gaze.

He glanced at his watch. "It's almost time for breakfast to be served," he whispered. "Use the back stairway to get to your room. Grab your things and meet me in the lobby."

As Becca hurried to the rear stairway, Luke retrieved his backpack from his room and descended the grand stairway to the main lobby and sitting area.

"I hope you slept well last night," the owner said when Luke approached the reception desk.

"The room was very accommodating, but we're going to have to get on the road today and travel farther west to meet up with a friend."

"I hope you'll come back again."

"I'm sure we will."

Just then, Becca stepped into the main lobby area. "The room was lovely." She handed the key to the woman behind the desk. "Thank you."

"You folks are getting an early start. Can I fix you a to-go breakfast box?"

Luke held up his hand. "That's not necessary."

"At least grab a cup of coffee. The carafe and fixings are on a service cart near the dining room."

He glanced at Becca. "Coffee sounds good."

Together they filled large disposable cups with coffee. Becca kept hers black while Luke loaded his with sugar and cream, then topped both cups with plastic covers.

"Ready?"

Becca nodded. "As long as Hank isn't around," she whispered.

They waved to the owner. "Thanks again."

"See you on your next trip to town," she said with a friendly wave.

Once outside, Luke peered along the street and at the surrounding buildings, searching for Hank and the security guard's SUV. Seeing no one in the area, they hurried to the rear of the B and B, where Luke's pickup was parked.

Luke's stomach twisted when he spied a paper stuck under his windshield wiper blade. He pulled it loose and stared at the message written in red ink.

Leave town and don't come back. Troublemakers like you could end up at the bottom of the lake.

Becca peered over his arm and gasped. "Hank's becoming more aggressive. Should we talk to the sheriff?"

"Not after what the dispatcher said last night. I have a feeling it's a good-old-boy network in town."

He saw Becca's confusion.

"That means they're all pals and hang out together,"

Luke explained. "The sheriff won't do anything to Hank, no matter if he wrote the note or not."

"Then you think Waterbend's law enforcement is corrupt?"

"I don't know, but I don't want to take any chances when we're the newcomers in town, and we've already received so much pushback about being here. Let's head to Miss Hattie's house and say a quick goodbye."

When they arrived at the kindly woman's home, Luke knew something was wrong, as the curtain on the side panel pulled back before the door opened. Instead of a smile, Hattie wore a worried expression and seemed nervous as she peered up and down her quiet suburban street.

"Come inside quickly." She motioned them into the foyer and grabbed their hands after closing the door behind them. "A man pounded on my door last night. I should have glanced outside first, but I was thinking of you folks being in town, and I believed you had come back for some reason."

"Who was it, Hattie?" Luke saw the tension on the sweet woman's face.

"A big man, dark eyes, bald head. He was wearing a dark jacket."

Becca gasped. "The bald-headed man."

"He wanted to know about Mr. Thomas and what he had given me for safekeeping. I explained I didn't have anything, but he seemed angered by my response even though it was the truth."

"Did he hurt you?"

"He shoved his way inside. I fell against the couch. That's when I picked up the crystal vase." She pointed to a heavy cut-glass ornament on the coffee table. "He backed off a bit then and told me to stay calm, which was impossible, as I was worked up."

"I'm sorry, Hattie. I did this to you."

"It wasn't you, Luke. It was the man who wanted something that belonged to Mr. Thomas. He mentioned papers and computer files, but I told him to get out of my house."

"Did he mention Becca or me?"

Her gaze darkened. "I didn't want to tell you, but he asked if you were staying here. He needed to talk to you. I told him you didn't live in town anymore, but he knew you had come back, and he got mad that I wasn't telling him everything."

"I have a gut feeling he didn't leave peacefully."

"I think you would have been right if I hadn't called Nate earlier in the day. I told him you were coming for lunch, and he said he wanted to see you. Nate had driven here after work. He has a key to my house, so he let himself in and found the man in the living room with me brandishing the vase as if it was a weapon."

"What happened?"

"My Nate's a big man, and he works out to keep in shape. The bald man started making excuses for why he was here, saying it was all a mistake, which Nate didn't believe for a minute. The bald man ran out of the house faster than you could say 'good riddance.'"

"Where's Nate now?"

"He's getting air in my tires and filling up my fuel tank while I finish packing."

"You're leaving town?" Becca grabbed Miss Hattie's hand.

"I'm staying with Nate in Nashville until this whole thing is over."

"Can we help you pack?" Luke looked at Hattie and then at Becca who nodded in agreement.

"I'm almost done. Nate will be back in a few minutes. I know he'd like to see you, but your safety is more important. Leave town now, Luke." She squeezed Becca's hand even more tightly. "You don't want anything to happen to this sweet lady."

Luke hugged Hattie. "I'm sorry about last night."

"You're not to blame, Luke. Do you even know who the bald man is?"

Becca stepped closer. "He appeared at my house after Mr. Thomas was killed and asked the same questions he asked you."

"About the computer files and notes?"

Becca nodded. "*Yah*. It must have something to do with Mr. Thomas's project. It seems he took his data with him when he left town."

"Maybe so, and maybe the Institute believes that work belongs to them, so they're searching for him and the bald man is as well. Does he work for the Institute?"

"That seems doubtful, unless there are two factions within the Institute that are working against each other."

"Which worries me even more. I'll be praying for both of you." Hattie opened her arms and wrapped Luke in a warm embrace that took him back to his childhood, when Miss Hattie had showered him with the attention he didn't get from his mother.

"Thank you for all you did for me when I was growing up, Miss Hattie. You were a source of love that I needed."

"Your mother loved you, but in her own way. And you were the apple of your father's eye, as the good book says."

Luke didn't know the quote from Scripture, but he would look it up after he took Becca home.

"I'll call you when all this is resolved."

She raised her brow. "Call me anyway, even if it isn't resolved. I don't want to lose track of you again." She hugged Becca. "And take care of this sweet lady. She's a gem, Luke."

Becca's cheeks pinked at Hattie's words as she accepted her hug and responded in kind.

"Now, you two get going before those bad men start looking for you again."

"I don't want to leave you until Nate gets back." Luke peered out the front window.

At that moment, the sound of a door opening in the rear of the house startled them. Luke stepped protectively in front of Becca and Miss Hattie.

"Grandma, is Luke here?"

"Nate!" Miss Hattie patted her chest. "You frightened all of us. We're in the living room."

A big man hurried into the room. He had short-cropped black hair and a gaze as warm as Hattie's. "Long time no see, dear friend." He opened his arms and wrapped Luke in a bear hug.

Both of them slapped each other's shoulders and then stepped back to exchange wide smiles.

"This is a terrible way to have to meet after all these years," Luke said once he had introduced Becca. "I hate bringing danger to your grandmother."

"I've kept in touch with friends in town who say bad things are happening at the Institute. Your father left at the right time. That upset them, and they locked down even more tightly after he was gone."

"I saw some magazine articles about a product they want to release that has to do with crop production."

Nate nodded. "All I know is that they were throwing big money into the promotion of the product before it was ready for market in order to build up interest. I think they were trying to attract buyers and create some type of a bidding war."

"Becca and I stopped by the Institute yesterday, but a security guard made it clear we weren't welcome. My one wish was to get a better look at the home where we lived." He glanced down for a moment before returning his gaze to his friend. "That home holds the last memories of my father. I was a kid, and maybe I didn't see everything that went on, but getting a close view of the house would allow me to put the past into perspective and maybe heal a bit of the hole in my heart."

Nate's gaze was filled with understanding. "Where are you headed next?".

"To the senior rehab center in Hartwell. We want to talk to Dad's former lab assistant."

"You can stop at the Institute on the way to Hartwell. You'll pass Hillside Road, which runs along the crest of the hill that the Institute backs up to."

"You mean the hill on the far side of the lake?"

"That's right. There's a turnaround where you can pull off the road. Leave your car there and hike down the hill to the stream. From the water's edge, you'll have a good view of the homes around the lake. I've hiked there a number of times and have never seen security. They're focused on the entrances and the area around the main laboratory."

Luke and Nate exchanged phone numbers and embraced once again. "After all this sabotage is over, we'll get together for a reunion and catch up on lost time."

"Sounds good, Luke. You can count me in."

He glanced at Becca. "So nice meeting you. Keep this guy outta trouble, will you?"

She smiled. "It seems to follow us, but we're hoping everything will be resolved soon."

"It was good meeting you," Miss Hattie said to Becca. "Now, both of you, get out of town as fast as you can." She squeezed their hands. "And remember, I'm praying for you."

TWELVE

Becca kept watch for the white SUV as they left Waterbend. The turnoff to Hillside Road appeared on their right. Luke was quiet and pensive as he drove, no doubt recalling memories from his past.

"There's the clearing Nate mentioned." Luke pulled to the rear of the parking area where his truck was hidden by a stand of trees and helped her from the vehicle. Together they started down the steep incline.

Becca slipped on the fallen leaves and worried she was slowing Luke down. "Go ahead on your own. I'll wait for you here."

"Are you sure?"

She pointed to a nearby boulder. "If I hear anyone approaching, I'll hide behind that rock."

"It won't take me long, Becca, to get to the edge of the stream. From there I should be able to see my house."

Peering through the trees below, she could make out the lake in the distance. "Be careful, Luke."

"Don't worry. If something doesn't look right, I'll turn around, and we can get out of here fast."

Becca watched him climb down the hill but soon lost sight of Luke as the path curved through a thickly forested area. She waited for what seemed like a long time and worried something could have happened to him. Her anxiety increased until she decided the only way to calm her nerves was to follow along the trail he had taken. Slowly she eased her way down the incline. A stream ran along the foot of the hill, and the fenced area around the Institute appeared in the distance. The lake and brick homes were visible within the enclosure. She narrowed her gaze and tried to make out the details on the buildings.

An engine sounded. Her heart nearly stopped when she saw a security vehicle on the road that circled the brick homes inside the fencing. What worried her more was spotting Luke walking on a large fallen tree that lay across the stream.

He was using the tree as a bridge and making his way along the massive trunk, heading to the fenced enclave on the far side of the stream. Determined to maintain his balance, he seemed oblivious to the security vehicle.

Worried that Luke was heading straight into danger, she tried to get his attention.

"Luke," she called. "Luke, stop."

He turned, caught her eye and waved.

She pointed to the SUV zooming toward a padlocked gate. If the guard had the key, he could, no doubt, drive to the edge of the stream.

Luke saw the vehicle and turned too quickly to retrace his steps. He started to lose his balance, flailed his arms and jumped feet first into the water.

Becca hid in the underbrush. The car stopped at the fence, and the guard peered at the stream for a long moment. He made a call on his cell before he drove off again.

Once the guard had left the area, Becca crawled from the brush and headed to the stream to help Luke out of the water.

A sound caught her attention. She turned to look farther downstream and saw another security vehicle leave the fenced area through a different gate and race across a narrow wooden bridge. The car stopped, and the driver hopped out and ran toward the fallen tree where Luke was hiding.

As the guard drew closer, Becca's heart lurched. The security guard was Hank, who had accosted her the day before and followed them to Waterbend. The first guard must have notified him of their presence.

If Luke climbed from the water, he would run into the guard. Needing to distract Hank, Becca flapped her arms and ran away from the fallen tree.

Seeing Becca, Hank chased after her. She kept running, but she struggled to make her way through the thick underbrush. Her heart pounded with the exertion, and her breath was labored, but she pushed on.

The branch of a tree brushed against her arm. She shoved it aside, seeing the scratch and the red pinpoints of blood where the prickly bark had dug into her skin.

She slowed for a moment and gulped in a lungful of air. Her foot caught on a root as she started off again. She landed on her hands and knees, scrambled to her feet and continued forward. The path became steeper, and she peered at the stream below, knowing if she lost her footing again, she would tumble down the ridge and into the water.

She could hear Hank's labored breath behind her. Glancing over her shoulder, she saw him tangled in the underbrush. While the guard slapped at the prickly branches that tugged at his clothing, she turned ninety degrees to her right. Leaning down, she dug her fingers into the soil to keep from slipping backward as she climbed up the steep incline.

The guard let out a cry of exasperation before breaking free from the brush. Needing to hide, she crawled behind a boulder and flattened herself against the jagged rock. Her heart pounded fast and hard, and she feared the guard would hear what sounded like a diesel engine in her ears.

Keep him moving along the stream, dear Gott, she silently prayed.

The guard's footsteps sounded on the path below her. Then he stopped. She heard his ragged intake of air. Her side ached from the exertion. Her legs were weak, and she doubted she could outrun him.

Seconds ticked by. The sharp edge of the boulder dug into her back. Fear gripped her. If he sneaked up to her, she wouldn't be able to flee.

Her mouth was dry as cotton. She fisted her hands and prayed. *Please,* Gott, *save me and save Luke.*

A twig snapped. She turned her head and listened. From his heavy footfalls, she determined Hank was backtracking and heading to the fallen tree. She could only pray Luke had climbed out of the water by now.

Gulping air, she gazed around the rock. Seeing nothing, she remained stationary for another couple minutes and then began to climb again. Every few feet, she glanced back, expecting to see Hank. Her muscles ached, and she sighed with relief when she arrived at the top of the hill.

The road lay ahead of her. She glanced right. Luke's truck would be a long way down the road. She gasped for air, then, hearing the approach of a vehicle, she hid in the underbrush, fearing the security guard's SUV would appear at any moment.

As the vehicle came into view, she nearly cried for joy when she saw the red pickup.

Luke jumped from his truck and wrapped her in his arms. "I thought he'd grabbed you."

"He almost did." She touched his shirt. "You're dry."

"The stream wasn't deep. I had taken off my shoes and left them at the side of the water so they didn't get wet, either. I lost sight of you and thought you had returned to the truck. When I didn't find you there, I decided to drive along the hilltop in hopes of spotting you on the way."

He gave her another hug. "I'm so glad I found you. Now, let's get out of here."

They hurried to the pickup and climbed in. Becca sighed with relief as she buckled her seat belt.

"Did you see your house?"

He nodded. "It's not as grand as I envisioned, and I realized a house isn't necessarily a home. I need to focus on the good memories rather than embellish anything that was a child's daydream. I trust Miss Hattie. She told me my father loved me." He glanced at Becca. "You did as well. I have to believe he did. With time, I feel sure my heart will heal."

She squeezed his hand as they left Hillside Road and turned on to the road to Hartwell.

"You're at a better place, so everything that happened at the lake was worth the effort." Becca squeezed Luke's hand, but a web of fear tangled around her spine.

She knew the security guard would continue to come after them. He was working for the Institute, which thought Luke's dad had stolen data belonging to them. Becca and Luke had to prove them wrong. Somehow.

Luke had been terrified when he'd arrived at his parked truck and hadn't seen Becca. His only thought was that he had to find her before Hank did.

Seeing her along the side of the road had sent him into

a state of euphoria that was short-lived. She had, once again, been in imminent danger because of Luke's quest to find out more about Andy Thomas. Although he appreciated the information Hattie and Carol had provided, he was worried about Hank and his knack for showing up when they least expected. Luke had to be more careful.

He glanced at Becca and his heart swelled in his chest. Never before had he felt such a mix of emotions when he'd been with someone. The feelings had taken him by surprise and wouldn't let go. Becca was special. Very special. She was also in danger, and Luke needed to do everything in his power to keep her safe.

THIRTEEN

When they arrived at the senior rehab center, Luke parked in the rear. He and Becca rounded the building and hurried to the main door.

He glanced at the Welcome sign and the visiting hours and gave Becca a thumbs-up. "Visiting hours started fifteen minutes ago. Our timing is perfect."

She raised her brow. "God's timing."

"I don't understand."

"God's timing is perfect, Luke."

He chuckled softly. "I guess you're right, but I never thought of it like that."

"When you pray and ask for God to provide something, His timing is always perfect."

He grabbed Becca's hand and wrapped his fingers through hers before he held the front door open for her.

A lady with short black hair and a wide smile sat behind a reception counter and welcomed them to the facility. She pointed to the open three-ring binder on the counter. "Would you folks sign in with your names and the time you arrived and who you plan to see? When you leave, we ask that you sign out as well."

Luke signed them in, using the alias names they had registered with at the B and B. "We're here to see Joseph Morris."

The receptionist pointed to a distant corridor. "Joe's room is the third on the left. If his door is closed, knock before you enter."

Luke and Becca hurried to where the woman had pointed. Mr. Morris's door was partially open. Luke knocked, then peered into the room. An aide was feeding an older man, who was propped up in bed.

She smiled widely and motioned them into the room. "Looks like you have company, Joe."

His face sobered as he glanced at Luke.

"Are you folks friends from the Institute where Joe worked?" the aide asked.

"Joe was a friend of my father's." Luke stepped toward the bed. "Hello, Mr. Morris. It's been a long time, sir."

The nurse removed the breakfast tray from the hospital table. "I'll give you some privacy. Joe had a problem in the night, so he might not feel like talking, although visiting with company is always a nice change of pace."

Luke glanced at Becca. She nodded as if understanding his request and followed the nurse into the hallway.

Hopefully Becca would find out about Joe's problem. The man stared at Luke and attempted to smile. Luke took his hand.

"Remember Andrew Thomas's son, Luke? You brought me an autographed picture of Tom Glavine. Dad hung it in my bedroom."

His mother hadn't packed the photo when they left town, and Luke wondered where the picture could be now.

"That photo was a treasure," Luke continued.

"Andy?"

Luke leaned closer, realizing the older man's confusion. "Andy was my father. I'm Luke. Do you know anything about my father's project and where he might have put his papers and data?"

"I didn't tell him. Like you said, they were after the data."

Luke leaned closer. "Who was after the data?"

He mumbled a name.

"Can you say that again?"

Joe closed his eyes and appeared to be falling asleep.

Luke patted his hand. "Open your eyes, Joe. You wanted to tell me about the data. Was it someone at work?"

The older man nodded. "Bruce."

"Bruce worked with you?"

"Not...not with... CLO."

"The chief laboratory officer?" Luke asked. "You and my dad worked for him. Isn't that right, Joe?"

He nodded, then pointed to a nearby chest of drawers. The top of the dresser was covered with baseball memorabilia. "Gave him false data."

"You gave him the false data I prepared before I left town?" Luke said as if he was his father.

Joe nodded.

"Did Bruce know I had altered the data?"

Joe put his finger to his lips. "Shh."

"Thanks for keeping it under wraps, Joe. I could always depend on you, my friend."

Although his eyes were heavy with fatigue, Joe smiled.

"What about last night?"

"A bald man... My blood pressure." He raised his thumb.

Luke leaned closer. "Your blood pressure went up?"

"Injection." Joe's voice was little more than a whisper.

"He gave you a shot?"

Joe nodded and patted his heart.

"What did the bald man want?"

"Data."

"Just like Bruce?"

"Hidden—"

Luke tried to piece together what Joe had said. "Hidden data? Where's it hidden?"

Again, he raised his hand and pointed toward the bedside table.

Luke noticed the photo of Tom Glavine. Although smaller in size, it was the same shot of the major league star as Joe had given Luke when he was a boy.

Joe stretched out his hand again. "Data."

"The picture?"

Luke held it up to Joe. "Is this what you wanted?"

He pointed to the metal stand. "Off."

Luke turned the photo over and tugged on the stand, surprised when it pulled away from the actual frame.

Joe reached for it again. "Inside."

Luke peered into the area behind the photograph. Something was taped to the inside of the frame. He stuck his hand in the narrow space and pried the tape from the object, then turned the frame over. A small metal device dropped onto Joe's bed.

His eyes widened. "Data."

Luke's heart pounded, realizing the small object was a computer flash drive. He held it up for Joe to see. "The data is on the flash drive?"

The older man smiled weakly. "Half. My half."

Had Luke's dad split the information to prevent the entire project from being stolen?

Luke patted the older man's hand. "You did a good job protecting the information, Joe. I'll keep it now so you don't have to worry."

Becca had met up with the nurse in the hallway.

"You said a man was here last night?"

"That's right. A big, muscular guy with a bald head.

He knew Joe had worked at the Institute, and he mentioned being a baseball fan as well."

The nurse shrugged. "Joe's been doing fairly well recently, but something must have happened during the bald man's visit. When I returned to check on Joe, he was visibly agitated and had a nosebleed."

She rubbed her hands together. "I should have known something was wrong. Joe's on warfarin, a blood thinner. This morning, his arm wouldn't stop bleeding when I drew his blood. The head nurse ordered an INR, and it was much too high. She notified his doctor. I've got a special spot in my heart for Joe, so I'm staying until the doc lets us know what he wants done. He may want Joe sent to the hospital."

"What is the INR?"

"A lab test that indicated his blood was too thin. He was also experiencing heart palpitations and increased blood pressure."

"Could someone have given him more anticoagulant?"

"No one here would give a patient meds without going through the dispensing nurse. If Joe received additional medication, it had to have come from an outside source."

Becca nodded. "Such as a visitor."

The nurse's eyes widened. "You think the bald man did something to cause Joe's bleed?"

"I'm merely saying it is a possibility."

Becca started back to Joe's room and stopped short, seeing a man walk down the hallway. Her heart nearly stopped. *Hank!*

The security guard looked as surprised as she felt. He lunged forward, grabbed her arm and twisted it behind her back.

"Let me go," she demanded. She tried to jerk free, but he held it even more tightly.

Pain radiated down her spine.

The nurse's eyes were wide. "Sir, you need to leave immediately."

Becca threw herself against the wall. He still had hold of her arm and smashed her face against the cold tile. Raising her free hand, she reached for the fire alarm on the wall.

He jerked her away from the wall. "No, you don't."

The nurse charged into him. He released his hold on Becca. She opened the glass window on the alarm and pulled the lever. The loud wail of the fire alarm sounded throughout the assisted living facility.

Luke raced out of Joe's room, saw the chaos in the hallway and tackled the guard. He fell back against the nurse's cart. Becca grabbed a fire extinguisher off the wall, activated the foam and directed it at Hank, hitting him in the face. He flailed his arms and slipped on the wet floor.

Luke grabbed Becca's hand. She dropped the extinguisher, and they raced for the back door.

Sirens screamed in the distance as they climbed into Luke's truck. He gripped the steering wheel white-knuckled and turned on to a side road just as the fire trucks pulled into the parking lot.

"Did you learn anything from Joe?" Becca asked, breathless.

Luke pulled a flash drive from his pocket. "This has some of the data but not all. Evidently my dad only left a few notes at the lab. Joe had a bit more information but not enough to reproduce his product."

"So we need to find the rest of the data?"

"If we want to know about his product—otherwise it will have died with him."

FOURTEEN

Becca's heart continued to pound at a rapid rate as they raced along the narrow road. She glanced back, expecting to see Hank's SUV.

"It will take him a few minutes to get to his car," Luke assured her. "We need to hole up someplace safe."

"Let me plug something into your GPS."

Luke handed her his phone.

She pulled up the map app and tapped in Harmony Grove, then hit the prompt.

The computerized voice started to issue directions. "At the next stop sign, turn left on to Rural Route 12."

"You found someplace where we can stay?" Luke asked.

"Harmony Grove. The map app says the trip should take an hour and a half."

"What's there?"

"Lizzie and Caleb Lehman's farm."

"Your mother's sister and her husband?"

"That's right. We'll stop as we get into the Amish area and find some clothes for you."

His brow raised. "You don't like what I'm wearing?"

"In spite of your pickup, we'll dress Amish while we're at their farm and hide your truck in one of the barns. That way if Hank snoops around or if he's friends with law enforcement in the Harmony area, they won't think to check out an Amish farm and the Lehmans' visitors."

"You're sure your aunt and uncle will go along with this plan?"

"They're *gut* people, Luke. They raised two boys who lost their parents, but they never had children of their own. When my *mamm* and I would visit, they would spoil me, for certain."

He chuckled. "I doubt anyone could spoil you, Becca."

Which was exactly what Luke's dad would have said.

Both Becca and Luke kept watch on the road around them as they followed the GPS directions to Harmony Grove. They passed two sheriffs' deputies parked on the side of the road, but the officers appeared absorbed in their own conversations.

As they neared the Amish community, Becca relaxed slightly seeing the pristine farms. Wash hung on many of the clotheslines, farmers worked in the fields and children helped their mothers in the gardens. Buggies zipped along the road, and the Amish men tipped their heads in greeting as they passed. The rhythmic clip-clop of the horses' hooves soothed Becca even more, and she breathed in the fresh air and kept her eyes on the placid scenery.

"It's lovely country," Luke said as if he, too, enjoyed the beauty of the area. "There's a peace here that I sensed in Mountainside as well."

"*Yah*, the stability of an Amish community can be felt. At home, I never tune in to the horses' hooves on the pavement as the buggies pass, but after being in Waterbend, the sound now comforts me."

"Your aunt and uncle will be glad to see you."

"Which reminds me that I need to call Daniel." Using Luke's cell, she tapped in the number to her brother's business phone and left a message on his voice mail.

"Luke and I plan to stay with Aunt Lizzie and Uncle Caleb for a few days before I return home. Do not worry, Daniel. I am fine."

She disconnected and pointed to a secondhand store on the next corner. "Pull into that parking lot. You should be able to find a pair of britches, along with a shirt and suspenders, inside."

"Plus a hat?"

She nodded, pleased that he realized Amish men wore hats outside as they worked, straw hats in summer and black felt in the colder months.

A horse was tied to the hitching post. Luke parked a few yards from the buggy and hurried around his truck to open Becca's door.

She smiled. "Are all *Englisch* men so attentive?"

"I have no way of knowing, but they should be attentive to a beautiful woman who is riding with them."

"You are much too chivalrous, as the *Englisch* say."

"An old term. I can't imagine Amish men talking about being chivalrous."

"Your father said I should look for a chivalrous man. I told him the term had gone out of use along with the Knights of the Round Table."

"You read stories about the Knights?"

She laughed as she stepped to the pavement. "Of course, as an impressionable young teen. My friends and I would often talk about finding our own knight in shining armor."

"Did you?" His gaze intensified.

"Did I what, Luke?" She hoped to change the direction of this conversation.

"Did you find your knight, a *gut* man, as you say, who would love you and care for you?"

Her cheeks warmed, and she swatted playfully at his hand that reached for hers.

"To answer your question, no, I never found my knight. Your father said Amish men should have been lined up on the porch of the bakery. But then, your father always had nice things to say."

"He was truthful, Becca. Amish men should have flocked to your door."

"I fear they thought I was too independent. Besides, I am happy living my own life. A man is not a necessity."

He reached out and tucked an elusive strand of hair behind her ear. "Love is not about necessity, Becca. It is about giving your heart to another and wanting the best for that person. It is living together as one."

"You make me blush with such talk, Luke. You did not have *gut* role models in your home life. How can you be so sure of what love is?"

He shook his head. "It is a feeling that seems as basic as the need for food and water. Love brings joy to a person's heart. Without that special someone, a person can become hardened and bitter."

"Are you saying I'm a bitter person?"

"On the contrary—I'm saying you're very special."

"Oh, Luke!" Did he not realize that Amish and *Englisch* did not mix, and as chivalrous as he was, she could not become interested in a man who was *Englisch*— unless she decided to leave her faith. She glanced again at the surrounding area. At the present time, she was filled with a sense of homecoming, which meant she could not allow herself to be attracted to Luke. As wonderful as he was, he was not Amish.

Luke sorted through the racks of clothing and found two pairs of Amish trousers and two shirts, one white and one blue. Becca checked to ensure they were made to Amish stipulations. She found a set of suspenders and a black felt hat that was new. Luke went into the dressing room as an *Englischer* and stepped out feeling totally Amish, although the suspenders made him wonder if he would ever get used to the tug on his shoulders.

He settled the hat on his head and wiped the brim, enjoying the feel of the felt and the way it fit. If he remained in an Amish community for very long, he would grow his hair a little longer and think about a beard. As Becca explained, Amish men who were married grew beards, but older men, even if they weren't married, often had beards as well.

Becca looked perplexed when he exited the dressing room.

"Is something wrong?" he asked, seeing the furrow in her brow.

"You surprise me, Luke."

"In what way?"

"You look Amish."

"Isn't that the plan?"

"*Yah*, but I did not expect such a transformation. Except—" She stepped closer. "Turn around, please."

"It's the suspenders, right?"

"*Yah*, they need to be loosened just a bit. They are to hold up your pants but not to be so tight that you cannot move."

He saw the twinkle in her eye and smiled. "Looks like I flunked suspenders."

"They can be easily adjusted."

He felt her fingers sweep against his back with a lightness that made his chest constrict.

The clerk headed toward them just as Becca completed the adjustment.

"This is a *gut* fit," the young Amish clerk said with a nod of his head. "You wish to wear them out of the store?"

"Yah." Becca then added something in the Pennsylvania Dutch dialect Luke couldn't understand. Becca and the clerk chuckled, making Luke wonder if he was the reason for their laughter.

When the young man returned to the counter to help another person, Luke glanced at Becca. "Do I stand out like a sore thumb?"

"Meaning?"

"Meaning you and the guy were laughing. I wondered if I look totally out of place."

"You look very handsome, but that is not what I told the young man."

Luke tilted his head. "Handsome, eh?"

She nodded. *"Yah*, you are a finer man than any of the Amish men I have known."

"Yet you found that funny," he teased, seeing her cheeks grow pink.

Becca had a hard time covering up her embarrassment, and he didn't want to cause her discomfort, but he liked knowing that she found him attractive.

"I said the clothes fit you better, no doubt, than the person they were made for."

"And that was funny?"

"Because we both could imagine an Amish wife sewing the clothing and then her husband gaining weight from all the pies and cakes she baked, so she had to make new clothing in a larger size." Becca smiled. "This happens."

"At least I found clothes that fit. I'll pay for them and then we can be on our way."

"I will meet you outside. First, I must change, just as you have done. I will use the ladies' restroom in the gas station next door."

"Check to ensure Hank isn't around."

"I do not think he has come this far into Amish territory."

Luke reached out his hand and grabbed hers. "Be careful, Becca."

"*Yah.* You do not need to worry."

But Luke was worried. Even though they were some distance from Waterbend, he didn't trust Hank. The guy had tracked them before. He could track them down again.

FIFTEEN

Once Becca had slipped into her Amish dress and apron and had brushed her hair into a bun and pinned on her *kapp*, she hurried back to Luke's truck. He was standing by the passenger door and blanched when he saw her.

"Is something wrong?"

He shook his head. "Not a thing is wrong. It is just that you look different in the Amish clothing."

"Different? In what way?"

"I'm not sure I can express the change." He glanced at her dress and then up at her face. "*Feminine* is probably the best word to describe you."

"Did I not look like a girl when I wore jeans and a sweater?"

"Well, ah, yes, of course you did." He seemed tongue-tied and embarrassed, which wasn't like Luke. Usually he was in control, but at the moment he appeared to be a young Amish guy who didn't know what to say.

She smiled sweetly. "We had better return back in your truck and keep driving."

"How much longer until we get to your aunt and uncle's house?"

"It shouldn't be far, but I do not know which roads to take after we get to Harmony Grove. Plus, we must make certain to arrive without being followed by Hank."

Luke opened the passenger door and offered his hand to help Becca climb into the pickup.

Once she was settled, he rounded the truck and slipped behind the wheel. "Which way?"

She pointed toward town. "We'll need to stop at one of the stores for directions. The GPS does not show the rural farm roads in this area."

Harmony Grove was a small town with a main thoroughfare and a number of intersecting streets. Becca glanced at each of the roads, and Luke did the same. They were getting accustomed to checking around them lest someone in an SUV from the Institute be nearby.

"The Sweet Shop on the corner will be a good stop. Parking's in the rear. You stay with the truck, Luke."

He raised a brow. "You're ashamed of the way I look?"

"Not at all, but if the clerk speaks in our own dialect, she might get suspicious if you don't understand what she's saying."

"Point taken, but be careful, Becca—and get some candy that I can give your aunt. My mother always told me to take a hostess gift when I visited someone."

"Let me off at the corner. I'll get the candy—"

"If they have nuts, get some of them as well." He shoved a number of bills into her hand.

"I have money."

"I'm sure you do, but this is a gift from me. After all, I'm the *Englisch* visitor."

"Who looks Amish." She opened the door. "It should not take me long."

The clerk, an Amish woman with rosy cheeks and big brown eyes, greeted Becca when she stepped inside. "May I help you?" she asked, speaking in Pennsylvania Dutch.

Becca answered as she pointed to the display case. "A

pound of mixed nuts, please. And a pound of assorted chocolates."

"The box makes a nice gift if you are buying the candy for someone else." The clerk indicated the boxed candy on a shelf closer to the window.

"The box will be perfect. *Danki.* Along with the nuts."

As Becca reached for the preboxed chocolate, her hand stopped in midair and she gasped. The white SUV driving down the main street was hard not to miss.

Her heart pounded. Hank had followed them somehow. Now he was in Harmony Grove, no doubt searching for them.

The clerk placed the bag of nuts on the counter next to the chocolates. Becca paid for them, all the while keeping her gaze on the road.

"Tell me," she said after the clerk had bagged her purchases, "is there a back road to Rural Route 23? I usually go through town, but I seem to recall a back way along some of the farm roads."

"*Yah*, this is true." The clerk pointed away from the main road where the SUV had driven and directed Becca through a number of turns that would eventually get them to the road on which her aunt and uncle lived. "It is not far," the clerk assured her.

The door to the shop opened, and an Amish woman entered with three children in tow who ran to the showcase and each pointed to a selection of candy. With the clerk's attention diverted to her new customers, Becca hurried outside.

Glancing each direction and relieved that the SUV was nowhere in sight, she turned the corner and headed toward the parking lot in the rear.

Footsteps sounded.

Her pulse raced. She glanced back. The security guard was walking behind her.

She increased her pace.

"Hey, ma'am," he called to her.

Her heart pounded even harder.

"Hey, stop a minute. I want to ask you a question."

She wouldn't fall for his tricks.

"You look like someone I know."

Someone you chased after at the lake and attacked at the assisted living center.

The parking lot was on her right, but she didn't want the guard to see Luke. She passed the lot and stepped into an Amish grocery store.

The clerk, a big man with a warm gaze, nodded a greeting.

"There is a man following me," Becca said in Pennsylvania Dutch. "He is acting strange."

"Yah?" The clerk left the canned goods he was shelving, stepped to the door and blocked the entrance when the security guard tried to enter.

The clerk asked him a few questions politely in the same Amish dialect, which stopped Hank in his tracks. He tried to glance around the clerk, but his big chest and burly physique kept the guard from noticing Becca hiding behind a row of dry goods—flour, cornstarch, sugar and seasonings—packaged in plastic bags. While the clerk continued to block Hank from entering the store, Becca headed out a side exit and wound her way to the parking lot, staying clear of the crowd of onlookers who had noticed the disturbance and gathered around the main entrance to the store.

Relieved to see Luke's pickup, she climbed into the passenger side. "Turn left. We'll take a back road."

"What happened?"

"I'll tell you after we leave town."

She ducked low in the seat so Hank wouldn't see her if he happened to have gotten free from the clerk and the gathering crowd.

"And the candy and nuts?"

She held up the bag. "I'm sure my aunt will enjoy them both."

If they could get to her aunt and uncle's house, Becca wanted to hole up and keep out of sight. The guard seemed to be everywhere they went. Had law enforcement notified the Institute about seeing a red pickup as they drove by their headquarters? If so, Becca and Luke might never be free of the security guard. Then she thought of the bald man. They needed to be free from him as well.

Luke wasn't a praying man, but he was worried about Becca's safety—and, truth be told, his own as well. Hank kept appearing no matter where they went, including this peaceful Amish community. At least now, Luke knew why.

"Guess what I found attached to the underside of my pickup while you were buying the candy and nuts?"

Becca shook her head. "I have no idea."

"A tracking device. My hunch is that Hank attached it the night we were at the B and B."

"That is why he kept following us."

"Exactly. But I crushed the device with my foot and threw it in a city dumpster. Hopefully Hank won't be able to find us from now on."

"Oh, Luke, that is good news, for sure."

He agreed, although out of habit, he looked in the rearview mirror and checked behind them to ensure they weren't being followed. As they drove along the rural road, Luke started to relax. Wearing Amish clothing was a first for Luke. No zippers, no collars, no belts. He wasn't sure everything fit the way it was supposed to, but Becca had approved of his outfit, so he must have done something right.

She looked pretty in her long dress. Her brow was tight with worry, but she seemed eager to be reunited with family. Luke couldn't blame her. From the little she had told him about her younger years, visits to the Lehmans had been delightful experiences, although they came too infrequently. With her mother gone, she probably longed to reunite, especially with her aunt.

"Aunt Lizzie and Uncle Caleb will enjoy getting to know you, Luke."

"Won't they wonder why a non-Amish person is wearing Amish clothing?"

"We will be honest and tell them what has transpired." She held up her finger. "I do not want them to worry, but they need to know about the bald man and his attacks and how Hank followed us all the way to Harmony Grove."

She glanced at the road behind them. "I am hoping that without the tracking device, he has traveled on to another area and is not following us now."

"I'll feel relieved when I can park the pickup in a secluded area and hole up on the farm. On a positive note, I'm interested in learning how your uncle works his land and what kind of seeds he buys. There will be much we can talk about."

"I am certain Uncle Caleb will enjoy sharing information with you. I told you, he and Aunt Lizzie raised two boys who lost their parents in a buggy accident. The boys are grown now, married with families of their own. They moved to Lancaster County, where their wives were from, and do not get to visit as often as they would like."

"Your aunt and uncle sound like good people."

She patted the hand he had rested on the console between the two front seats. "You are nervous, perhaps?"

Luke shrugged. "Only concerned that they will worry about you being involved with an *Englischer* as well as all the danger he has brought into your life."

"What do you mean by *involved*?"

Her gaze seemed innocent enough, but her question had Luke wondering what he should provide as an answer. "I would think most Amish women do not leave home and travel around the country on their own."

She thought for a moment. "*Yah*, that is correct, but I knew your father and wanted to help you learn more about him."

"Which I appreciate."

Becca pointed to the road on the right.

Luke made the turn and smiled at the pristine farm in the distance. "The red silo is their place?"

"*Yah*, Aunt Lizzie wanted people to be able to find their farm. Uncle Caleb said red was a bit pompous. He asked the bishop, who sided with my aunt."

"So he ended up painting his silo red." Luke smiled.

"Within a few months, my uncle admitted the color suited him as well."

"Tell me your uncle is a man who works hard and says little."

"I am not giving any information away. You must form your own first impressions."

Luke turned into their drive and braked to a stop near the farmhouse. The kitchen door opened, and an Amish woman, probably in her early fifties, stepped to the porch. Her brow was raised as she peered at the red pickup, then, narrowing her gaze, she leaned down to catch a better view of the occupants. In a flash, she let out a scream of pleasure and ran down the porch steps to meet Becca as she opened the passenger door and stepped out of the truck.

"What a wonderful surprise to see my dear niece," she said.

Becca's face was aglow. She stepped into the woman's outstretched arms, and the two ladies embraced for longer than Luke would have thought possible. He remained quietly at the side of his truck, feeling like an intruder at a family reunion.

At long last, Becca pulled back and held out her hand to Luke. "Aunt Lizzie, this is my friend Luke."

To her credit, Becca's aunt was gracious and offered him a warm welcome, although he picked up on a question flaring from the older woman's confused gaze.

At the very moment when Luke was wondering what to do next, a muscular man with a thick beard and black felt hat stepped from the barn. Seeing Becca, he tossed aside the pitchfork he was holding and hurried to hug her in an equally welcoming embrace.

Once again, Becca made the introductions. The two men shook hands, and Luke stood back as her uncle sized up the stranger who was wearing Amish clothing but was not of their faith.

"You must come inside and tell us about Daniel and his upcoming wedding," Becca's aunt said. "I have a pie cooling. We will cut it and enjoy it with coffee, *yah*?"

Becca nodded. "That sounds *wunderbar*, Aunt Lizzie, but we need to park Luke's truck in the barn, if you have room."

"*Yah*, this is not a problem."

Caleb hurried to the barn and directed Luke where he could park his truck. After the pickup was out of sight, Luke gathered their bags, closed the barn door and hurried back to the house.

Once in the kitchen, Luke smiled at her uncle, but the older gentlemen merely pointed to a chair at the table. *"Ga zitten."* Although Luke didn't understand the Amish dialect, he felt sure the uncle wanted him to sit.

Luke pulled out the chair they had indicated for Becca and helped to seat her at the table. Lizzie raised her brow and peered at her husband. Luke wasn't sure if she approved or not.

He had a sinking feeling that coming here had been a mistake, but when Becca's aunt placed a huge slice of apple pie in front of him and filled a mug with steaming coffee, he felt a bit more comfortable. Becca handed him the cream pitcher and sugar bowl with an understanding smile. He stirred sugar into the dark brew and hoped his sweet tooth didn't seem excessive before he poured the heavy cream into the mug. Once everyone started eating, he had to contain himself from smacking his lips at the rich cream and sweet coffee.

Becca's aunt picked at her slice of pie and then glanced at her niece. "You must tell us why you are here. There is a problem, *yah*?"

Becca nodded and glanced at Luke. He knew that her aunt and uncle needed the truth to be able to understand why they had to stay at their home for a few days. The seriousness of their situation flooded over Luke again as Becca recounted the explosion and his father's death.

"Ack," her aunt exclaimed. "You could have died as well."

Her aunt's words played heavily on Luke's heart as Becca shared about his father's request to notify his son if anything happened to him.

"And how did you end up here?" the older woman asked.

Luke explained about their visit to his dad's cabin and

his need to learn more about his father. "He was a scientist at the Tennessee Research Institute in Waterbend. Have you heard of it?"

Lizzie shook her head. "But this is not surprising. We live some distance from Waterbend. An *Englisch* research institute would not be something we would know about."

"From some articles we found at my father's home, the Institute planned to release a project he had developed on his own."

"He would have been cut out?"

Luke nodded. "That seems to be the case. Security around the Institute has become extremely tight, and a guard followed us. He evidently did not want us looking into my father's business."

"You think the people at the Institute arranged for the explosion?"

"They are a likely suspect. An explosion at a bakery would seem like a random malfunction in the stove or oven, whereas attacking him at his cabin would alert law enforcement to the fact that Luke's father was the target. Another man was hanging around and asking questions as well. He's not from the Institute, as far as we know."

The older Amish woman shook her head and tsked. "This sounds like a dangerous operation you have stumbled on to."

Becca sighed. "Which is the reason we must accept your hospitability for a few days."

"Of course. We will enjoy having you with us. You can sleep in the upstairs room where you stayed as a girl. Luke, there is a downstairs bedroom. It is small, but you should be comfortable there."

"I'm grateful." Luke touched his hand to his heart. "Thank you both for having us."

Becca's uncle had listened to their conversation but

said nothing until he finished eating his pie. He pushed his plate to the middle of the table and turned to Luke. "You are dressed Amish so these people will not find you, *yah*?"

Luke nodded. "Yes, sir. That's correct."

"You are a farmer?"

Taken aback by the question, Luke gulped. "I collect non-GMO seeds, study regenerative farming and work at an agricultural extension service to help farmers in the northwest section of Kentucky."

Caleb pursed his lips. "I have heard of this type of farming."

Luke started to explain a bit about what it encompassed until Caleb waved his hand. "This is what the Amish have done for generations."

His response surprised Luke.

The farmer stood. "You will come to the field with me. I will show you."

Becca smiled with encouragement as Luke scooted back from the table. He carried his plate and fork to the sink, rinsed them both, and left them on the counter. Finishing his coffee, he placed his mug on the counter as well.

Caleb grabbed his hat off the wall peg, and Luke did the same, then he glanced back at Becca. *I hope this goes well* was what he wanted to say, but he remained silent. Just as he had suspected, Caleb was a man of few words. He would let the farmer lead the discussion and wait until he was ready to talk. Luke hoped he wouldn't have to wait too long.

SIXTEEN

As soon as the men left the kitchen, Aunt Lizzie patted Becca's hand. "There is more you must tell me."

Becca nodded. She needed to explain about the journalist. "We found a phone number for a man who wrote an article in one of the farm magazines."

"Is it *Farmer's News*, by chance? Caleb subscribes and reads each issue cover to cover."

Surprised that her aunt would know the publication, Becca nodded. "Luke called the reporter yesterday and left a message, but he has not heard back."

"Perhaps you could contact him through the magazine?" Lizzie suggested.

"He freelances." Seeing her aunt's raised brow, she explained, "He does not write for one magazine but instead sends his articles to various publications. Once Luke meets with the journalist, he will drive me home to Mountainside."

Again, Aunt Lizzie patted her hand. "But going back to Mountainside is not something you are ready to do."

Becca appreciated how her aunt could read her heart, just as Becca's mother had always done.

Lizzie leaned closer. "You and Daniel are getting along?"

"*Yah*, of course. Daniel is a *gut* man, but he will soon marry."

Her aunt nodded. "He wrote us and invited us to the wedding."

"Which would be *wunderbar.*"

"You like this Katie he plans to marry?"

"She's a lovely woman, and we are friends, but I cannot stay and interfere with their new life together."

"It is often done, Becca. This would not be outside the norm."

"Perhaps not, but I do not want to infringe on their privacy, especially when they are newly married."

"You have a big heart like your mother, but where will you go?"

"At this time, I am not sure."

"You will come here. We have room, and I could use the help, plus you are family and would bring joy to this often-lonely farmhouse. We see the boys and their wives twice a year, and that is so special, but the rest of the year, our hearts long for more family."

Becca was touched by her aunt's offer. "Thank you, Aunt Lizzie. I will need to go home and help with the preparations for Daniel and Katie's wedding, but I will think about your generous offer. I would like to work in a bakery. Is there anything like that in town?"

"*Yah*—in fact, the local bakery is looking to hire a baker. It was a thriving business until Ellen Borntrager got married and left town with her new husband. Since then, the owner cannot keep up with the demand. Plus, he is good with business, but not so good with his baking. You would be a perfect fit for his bakery, and you could stay here as well."

A weight lifted off Becca's shoulders when she realized her worries about where to live once Daniel married had been resolved, especially if she could get a job at the bakery.

She would have a place to live and two wonderful people who would help her adjust to her new life. Seeing the bond between Daniel and Katie was wonderful, but it also made her realize how much she longed for a *gut* man to love. She could not explain to Lizzie how the Amish men in Mountainside fell short of the mark she had set for a husband. They were not bad men, but she could not see spending her life with any of them.

She cleared her plate and mug and took them to the sink. Glancing outside, she saw Luke and Caleb pointing to the pasture in the distance. Her heart thumped as she stared at him.

Her aunt came up behind her and placed her hand on Becca's shoulder. "You have given your heart to an *Englischer.*"

Becca shook her head. "You are wrong. He is a friend. Nothing more."

Lizzie put her finger under Becca's chin and turned her face to look at her. "You are confused and do not know how you feel, yet I can see it in your eyes. I understand love, and that is what I see."

"But if that is so, then what am I to do?"

"At your father's funeral, did you not mention your desire to know more about the world, as you called it? A world you could not explore while your father was alive."

"I… I thought that was what I wanted, and that was some of the reason I came to Tennessee with Luke. As much as I enjoy being with him, I had a sense of homecoming when we drove to your farm. Now here—" she looked again through the window at the acreage "—I realize it would be hard to leave my Amish roots."

"And Luke? What does he say?"

Becca glanced down. "He does not know how I feel, and I do not know how he feels, either."

Lizzie tilted her head and sighed. "It is *gut* that he is here to see the Amish way. Perhaps this will change his heart."

"He has a home in Kentucky and a job he plans to return to after he learns more about his father."

"Sometimes plans change," Lizzie said with a knowing gaze.

Becca doubted what her aunt had said would hold true. Yes, she had feelings for Luke, but he had never expressed any feelings for her.

Once again, she glanced outside to where Luke was talking to her uncle.

Becca had never given her heart to anyone. Until now.

Once Luke and Caleb were outside, the Amish man explained his own farming habits and tips, some of which were new to Luke.

"We help one another, *yah*?" Caleb told Luke. "There is much to do on a farm this size. When the boys were with us, they shared the work. Now I am alone. Forty acres is a *gut*-size farm for the Amish."

"You need help. Tomorrow, I'll work with you. Let me do some of the strenuous jobs."

Caleb shook his head. "We will work together. You can tell me what you learned in school, and I will tell you how we do it here."

He patted Luke's shoulder. "Perhaps you would like to see the ledgers I keep about my crops and production."

"Thank you, Caleb. I would enjoy that." Feeling drawn to the older man, Luke shared about his father's project that supposedly would increase crop production.

"This is much needed in that area," Caleb admitted.

"The government has cut back on subsidies, and the prices to farmers have not caught up to inflation. Store shelves are empty of some of the most basic products."

"It is the same in the *Englisch* world."

"The Amish take care of their own, *yah*? We will always have food, but for the *Englischers*, this is not so. I worry. The other Amish farmers worry as well. We can see production declining, and this is not *gut* for anyone."

Luke nodded in agreement. "The cost of fuel is another problem that increases the cost of products transported to market."

"We do not need the fuel except for our diesel generators that power some of our machinery, as well as the sawmills and water pumps. Still, the increased cost affects us as well. At least we keep our mares for transportation."

Luke looked at where the horses were grazing in a distant pasture. "Your mares are beautiful, plus, you have a number of draft horses."

"They are used to work the fields. They are strong and provide much of our labor."

"The *Englisch* could learn from you."

"And we from you." Caleb glanced at the sky then nodded. "You will be here tomorrow night?"

"If you don't mind us staying."

"It is not a problem. Tomorrow I will invite the local farmers to come here for dessert and to talk about farming. They will enjoy hearing what you have to say, and they will share their own experiences as well."

Luke couldn't believe his good fortune. An opportunity like that was so rare—to discuss farming with men who were one with the earth, who worked their farms as their fathers and grandfathers had done for centuries, would be such an opportunity.

"*Danki*, Caleb. I would enjoy such an evening."

"Then it is settled." He pointed to the house. "We will go inside and tell Lizzie to bake more pies tomorrow."

"How will she feel about having a surprise meeting?"

"She will enjoy baking with Becca at her side. She is lonely at times. I can tell this." He patted his chest. "It hurts my heart. We wanted a houseful of children, *yah*?"

Luke nodded. He could understand that desire. He, too, had thought about being a father one day, although he didn't know if he would be a good one or not. His adoptive father had always been too busy to spend time with Luke, but the memories that he wouldn't allow to turn his heart of his own father had made him wonder if he would be *that* type of a dad.

"Sometimes *Gott* does not provide that which we most want."

Luke understood Caleb's comment. He wanted answers about his father's project and the involvement of the Institute, but all that seemed to be lost to him unless the reporter, Rex, responded to his voice mail.

"Having Becca here is *gut* for Lizzie, so you must stay as long as you can."

Caleb's honesty was touching, and Luke felt for the nice couple who, just as Becca had said, were gracious and so welcoming.

The two men washed their hands at the pump outside. Caleb handed Luke a towel before they headed into the house.

Something simmered on the wood-burning stove and filled the kitchen with delicious smells that made Luke's mouth water. The pie had been wonderful, and he had no doubt that dinner would be as well.

Lizzie was busy mashing potatoes, and Becca was stirring a large bowl of what looked like custard. As a boy, Luke had loved Miss Hattie's banana pudding. His mother watched her weight and said the calories weren't worth eating, so after they left Waterbend he had never had banana pudding again. The slices of banana Becca placed on the top of the pudding confirmed his favorite dessert for the evening.

Suddenly he remembered the candy and nuts in the truck. He excused himself and hurried to the barn. Before he could open the barn door, a black sedan drove slowly along the road. Luke turned his head and glanced away from the road, glad for the large hat that helped to block his face from the driver. The car looked like the same vehicle that the bald man had driven, but it wasn't likely he could have followed them this far.

As much as Luke told himself that they were safe, he knew that the people who had killed his father and the bald man who had appeared soon thereafter were playing for keeps. Something big was involved in his father's project. Evidently it was an expensive venture that would bring in a lot of revenue to the group that released it for production.

Once the car had passed, he grabbed the Sweet Shop gifts for Becca's aunt, then closed the barn doors and hurried back to the porch. He turned to glance at the road and could still see the black sedan in the distance, driving slowly along the country road as if the driver was looking for something.

If it was the bald man, Luke knew what he was looking for: Becca and whatever information he thought his father had given her to keep.

A Bible. Maybe Luke should look at Scripture as well. He'd never had faith, but it was something that Miss Hattie had shared with him in his childhood. One time she took him to her church when his parents were out of town over the weekend. He'd loved the way the congregation came alive and praised the Lord.

His mother hadn't approved, and the next time Hattie babysat him, his mother asked her not to take Luke to church. He still remembered Miss Hattie's upset.

Although Luke didn't go to church with her after that, it hadn't stopped Hattie from talking about God and how much He loved Luke and would take care of him.

The words had touched his heart and given him a larger purpose in life, but, of course, all that ended when they left town. His mother didn't want to hear about what Miss Hattie had said, and Luke soon realized what he had learned about God needed to be kept inside him. He had thought the memories would vanish over time, but this evening, surrounded by the peace and calm of this farm and the fresh air and pink twilight sky, he realized all those memories had returned.

Yes, he would read his father's Bible after he drove Becca home. He would need a faith to bolster his spirits when he had to say goodbye to her. Leaving her in Mountainside would be so hard. It wasn't what he wanted to do, but some things had to be, which was what his mother had told him as they drove away from the Institute that night. She said he needed to be a man instead of a little boy, but at ten years of age, he hadn't had the power to stop the tears, so he had pretended to nap in the back of the car when, in reality, he had cried himself to sleep— the first of many times over the next few years, until he realized crying didn't solve anything and that he had to be a man because his father was gone from his life. He had thought God was out of his life as well, but now he realized he was wrong. God hadn't left Luke, but Luke had left God when he left his father and Miss Hattie.

SEVENTEEN

Helping Aunt Lizzie brought back so many memories. Becca could still hear the laughter in the kitchen as her mother and aunt talked of their childhood and growing up in Ethridge.

In the short time Becca had been with her aunt today, she had sensed the tension and concerns of the trip easing, replaced with an inner peace she hadn't experienced in a long, long time.

What her aunt had said about Luke still echoed in her mind so that her heart lurched when Luke followed Caleb inside, only to turn around almost immediately and head to the barn.

Becca had glanced through the window over the sink, pretending to be rinsing the spoon she had used to stir the pudding. He had stopped momentarily and then stared after a dark sedan that had slowly driven by the house. Becca's heartbeat picked up a notch as she thought of the bald-headed man's sedan and his heinous actions when he was trying to uncover information about Luke's father's papers.

The same man had more than likely visited Joe Morris at the care facility, but could he be in Harmony Grove as well? Surely he had returned to his own home, wherever that was.

Her concerns eased when Luke returned to the kitchen, hung his hat on the wall peg and sheepishly placed the box of chocolates and bag of mixed nuts on the counter next to where Aunt Lizzie was working.

"Forgive me for almost forgetting to give these to you," he said. His smile exuded charm and made her heart pound all the more, but this time with attraction for the sweet *Englischer* who looked totally Amish in his thrift-shop clothing.

"What is this?" Lizzie's smile widened, and a twinkle gleamed in her pretty eyes. "You brought this for me?"

Luke nodded, and for a second Becca caught sight of how precious the young Luke must have been to have stolen Miss Hattie's heart.

"My mother always gave the hostess a little gift when she visited."

"Your presence here is gift enough, Luke, but I appreciate your thoughtfulness. *Danki!*" Lizzie glanced at her husband and niece. "After dinner, we will enjoy both treats."

She placed the potato masher in the sink and carried the large bowl of fluffy potatoes to the table. "Now we will eat."

Becca sat at the same place reserved for her when she was a girl. Her aunt had pointed Luke to the chair directly across from Becca, and his smile as he helped her scoot her chair into the table and then settled himself across the way made her feel like a young schoolgirl again. Lizzie must have noticed Becca's expression, because she had an impish smile that appeared hard to wipe away even when she lowered her head in prayer.

Becca looked down, then glanced across the table, pleased to see that Luke had closed his eyes and seemed to be communicating in some way with the Lord. She recalled his curt comment about not reading the Bible when she had first mentioned the book his father had given her for safekeeping. Something had changed in Luke, she felt certain, especially as he continued to keep his eyes closed even when Lizzy and Caleb patiently waited for their guest.

Luke glanced up and widened his eyes. "Sorry, I got carried away."

"One can never pray too long," Lizzie said as she passed the mashed potatoes to her husband, who har-rumphed.

"Although a too-zealous prayer can lead to a cold dinner, which is not to my liking," he grumbled good-naturedly.

"Everything looks delicious, Aunt Lizzie. You always were an amazing cook and gracious hostess."

"It is not difficult when delightful people are gathered around the table."

Uncle Caleb was quiet as he ate. He had seconds on the mashed potatoes and roast and then placed his knife and fork on his plate and scooted his chair back. "Luke and I have planned a gathering here at the house tomor-row evening."

Aunt Lizzie stopped her fork midbite and waited for her husband to explain.

"Luke has schooling on some new farming techniques that I think our neighbors would benefit from hearing about. In turn, they can share their own knowledge on crop production."

Lizzie returned her fork to her plate and smiled at Luke. "I am certain the men would like to hear what you have to say, Luke. I planned to bake tomorrow morning." She patted Becca's hand. "And I will have a helper. We will serve apple pie and sugar cookies along with coffee."

"I will pass the word that we will meet at seven o'clock," Caleb said. "That will give us at least two hours to be together before the neighbors return home."

Becca raised her brow at Luke and nodded ever so slightly to let him know that her aunt and uncle seemed pleased by what he planned to do.

Caleb eyed Luke askew. "From what you told me today, your farming ideas are *gut*. Have you thought of joining our community?"

Becca was surprised by her uncle's brazen statement. Luke appeared to be surprised as well.

"Ah, no, sir. I was never around the Amish until I met Becca, and that was only a few days ago."

"Time does not matter. It is what you feel in your heart."

Luke glanced at her as if he didn't know how to respond. Becca was equally flummoxed. Did her uncle mean how Luke felt about her or about the Amish lifestyle?

After dinner, Lizzie offered everyone a piece of chocolate and placed the nuts in a bowl for them to enjoy before she served the pudding, poured coffee and handed both to her husband. "We will eat our dessert in the living room." She glanced at Becca. "The night is mild. You and Luke should enjoy the porch swing."

Her aunt winked. Becca glanced at Luke to ensure he hadn't noticed the gesture, but he was focused on the large helping of banana pudding Lizzie had given him.

Becca steered Luke to the porch, where she placed her own plate on the small side table and then returned to the kitchen to retrieve the two mugs of coffee.

Handing one of the mugs to Luke, she smiled. "I added two spoonfuls of sugar and a dollop of cream. Real cream."

"I'm getting spoiled with these Amish desserts and rich cups of coffee."

"It is not spoiling you, Luke. It is sharing the *gut* nourishment the Lord provides."

"I'm beginning to understand a bit more about God, thanks to you, Becca."

She glanced at him, surprised. "I do not think we have talked much about *Gott*."

"Maybe not, but it is in the way you live your life. Your goodness is evident in everything you do."

"Yet I have questioned being Amish."

"Questions help us decide where we stand on issues. It helps us make good decisions, which you always do."

"Like your father, Luke, you see only the *gut*."

"I see only the *gut*, as you say, in you because you are a *gut* person." He put his plate and mug down and stepped closer. "And a pretty lady and a sweet, considerate and compassionate person."

She placed her mug on the side table and raised her gaze to meet his. "You are seeing with—" She hesitated. "What do the *Englisch* say about some kind of glasses?"

"Rose-colored glasses?"

She nodded. "That's it. You're seeing the color rose when really I am more a black-and-white person."

"Which means what?"

She shrugged. "I see everything either one way or the other, not halfway."

"You mean you can't be halfway Amish. You have to be either completely Amish or completely *Englisch*?"

"*Yah*, that is right."

"And what are you now?" A breeze fluttered a strand of her hair. Luke reached out and twirled it around his finger, then rubbed the back of his hand over her cheek.

She leaned into his touch without thinking and heard the sigh that escaped her lips.

Luke stepped closer. "Meeting you was the best thing that has happened to me in a long time. Perhaps my father planned to take that trip just so you would call me."

"I don't think he planned the explosion."

"But his death brought us together."

She nodded. "You are like him, Luke."

"I'll take that as a compliment."

"And the truth. I wish you could have gotten together this past year."

Luke placed his hand around her waist. "I've seen him through your eyes, which is a blessing. Before, I was focused on what my mother told me. She, of course, was not looking through rose-colored glasses." He tapped Becca's nose playfully. "She was focused on her own pain and whatever had transpired between them during their marriage."

"She was wrong to fill you with negative comments about your *datt*."

"I'm grateful to have learned the truth. Now, I hope we can learn more about his project and what transpired at the Institute to cause him to leave town and hide out in Georgia."

"Hopefully you will know something more when you talk to the journalist."

The clouds broke, and the moon appeared in the sky. Luke took her hand and guided her toward the edge of the porch where they could see the stars twinkling overhead.

"It's beautiful here." He glanced at the fields surrounding the house, barn and outbuildings. "Your aunt and uncle have created a wonderful farm that provides for their needs. If we had more farms like this one, I would not be as concerned about how the world will survive in the future."

"The Amish always say that *Gott* will provide."

He glanced down at her. "I never admitted that I had become lonely, living in my small house and spending my time on work and study."

"Did you not have a special girlfriend?" She held her breath, worried he might reveal more than she wanted to know.

"I never allowed myself time to socialize. Perhaps I was trying to make a difference and help people with the farming practices that seemed so important at the time. I wanted to change the world. Then I find out the Amish are using their own form of regenerative farming and have been successful for years and years."

"That does not diminish what you have studied and what you have shared with others."

Again, he gazed at the distant fields. "But seeing it put into practice makes me want to have my own farm and work my own fields the way Caleb and his neighbors do."

Becca's pulse picked up a notch. Was Luke saying he wanted to have a farm? An Amish farm?

"I am sure there is land to buy in the area."

"I must talk to Caleb."

He lowered his gaze to Becca. She saw the spark of excitement in his eyes. "Moonlight becomes you, Becca."

She smiled at the comment. "The night is perfect, *yah*?"

"One thing is lacking."

"Oh?" She was unsure what he meant.

"A lovely night, moonlight, a light breeze, stars above, a man." He moved closer. "A very beautiful woman."

Her heart pounded in her chest. His arms encircled her, powerful arms that surrounded her with such gentleness that she felt wrapped in softness and wanted to stay in his embrace forever.

"You said something is lacking—"

His gaze took her breath away. "A night like this is made for romance."

She could not take her eyes from his parted lips that lowered to her waiting mouth. Their lips touched in the gentlest of kisses that made her heart nearly jump out of her chest.

He drew her into his embrace, and she wrapped her arms around his neck. The world drifted into the background. Becca never wanted his kiss to end or the feeling of floating on air to stop. All her senses focused on Luke and the way he made her feel when she was wrapped in his arms.

"Oh, Becca," he whispered.

Before she could respond, the trill of his cell phone cut through the night.

Becca's euphoria plummeted. She drew back, confused about the 180-degree change the ring of the small mobile device could make.

Luke looked apologetically at her as he retrieved his cell from his pocket.

"Bad timing," he said as if he, too, were reeling from the interruption.

Her cheeks warmed, and she took a step back.

"It's the journalist." He glanced at Becca as if seeking her advice.

"You have to take the call."

"I'll put it on speaker so you can hear what Rex has to say."

Luke punched a button on his phone, then held it up between them. "This is Rex Bryant. I had a call from this number."

Luke introduced himself. "Andrew Thomas was my father."

"Was?" The journalist's voice was filled with question.

"My father died a few days ago in an explosion. I need to know who wanted him dead and why. I found a copy of the article you wrote in *Farming Life* on the project he created at the Institute. I also found your phone number in his desk."

"Look, I'm traveling and won't get home until late tomorrow night. Can we meet the following morning?"

"Will you be in Waterbend?"

"Not far from there. I'll call you that morning and give you specific details as to where we can connect. If you're smart, you won't mention this conversation to anyone. They found your father. Now they're after me. If they learn about our meeting, you will be in danger as well."

"I've been followed and attacked. Right now, I'm holed up and staying out of sight, but I'll be waiting for your call."

"You're not in Waterbend?" the journalist asked.

"Not currently, but I'll head there the morning after next. Unless you have time to talk now?"

"My cell's been overheating and losing battery power all too quickly. I'm worried my calls are being tapped. Face-to-face is safer. We'll plan to meet at 10:00 a.m. Stay on the outskirts of Waterbend until I call you. Security guards from the Institute are everywhere."

Luke disconnected and stared at Becca. "We'll meet with Rex, then I'll drive you home to Mountainside."

"But—" The moon disappeared behind the clouds, and they were surrounded by darkness. "What happens after that?"

"It depends on what Rex shares. More than likely I'll go back to Kentucky to sort out the information he provides. Plus, I need to determine what's on the flash drive Joe Morris had."

"You're going back to your house and your work?" She didn't remind him that he had mentioned being lonely there.

Becca would be lonely in Mountainside. She didn't want to say goodbye to Luke, but that's what he wanted, so she had no choice but to follow his lead.

A moment earlier, she had thought the future could involve both of them, but she was foolish to think an *Englischer*, even if he looked handsome in Amish clothing, would give up his way of life for the plain lifestyle.

Luke had needed her to learn more about his father. Rex would provide that last piece in the puzzle that showcased the real Andrew Thomas. Once the puzzle was completed, Luke would return home. So would Becca, but they would be miles and miles apart as well as culturally and religiously estranged.

Why had she been so gullible to think something could develop between them? Luke was a *gut* man, but he wasn't the man for her.

The next day, as Luke helped Caleb on the farm, he kept thinking of Becca in his arms and their lingering kiss that had rocked his world.

The journalist had called at the most inopportune moment, but knowing they would meet tomorrow was a relief. The problem was ensuring Becca's safety. If Caleb hadn't already invited the neighbors to his house this evening, Luke might have considered taking Becca home today and then rushing back to Waterbend in time for his meeting with Rex in the morning.

The journalist had mentioned that his own life was in danger and alluded to the fact that Luke could also be in danger. Luke already knew that he and Becca were in the security guard's crosshairs. The bald-headed man was another threat. Luke thought of the black sedan that had driven by Caleb and Lizzie's farm and was relieved that he had not seen a similar vehicle passing by again.

The bald man could still be in Mountainside, which was one reason Luke liked having Becca here with him. The other was that he enjoyed being with her and couldn't imagine how hard it would be to say goodbye. The only positive note was his father's cabin. As the only heir, Luke would need to prepare the cabin for sale, so he would return to Mountainside—and would see Becca again.

He wouldn't mention his plans to her at this time lest she adjust her own plans for her future to accommodate him. If she had moved on when he returned to her area, it would be hard to accept. What had Becca said about *Gott*'s will, as she called the Lord? The Amish trusted God to do what was best for each of them. Luke needed to embrace that concept as well.

Later that night, Luke tried to get Becca's attention as the buggies began to turn into the drive and park in the grassy area on the far side of the barn.

He had washed up and changed into a clean shirt and was eager to discuss farming, but he also wanted to steal a quiet moment with Becca. The memory of her in his arms continued to distract him.

His mind returned to farming as the Amish men started filling the living room. They were a good-natured group who seemed to enjoy life and the opportunity to gather together.

Luke had given presentations to various farming organizations, but to talk to a gathering of Amish men was a first. He was a bit anxious about how he would be received, but the men were rapt listeners and gracious in their attention. After talking for twenty minutes, he opened the floor to questions and then asked them to share how their farming practices differed from what he espoused. The discussion was lively and informative.

The meeting went well, and the Amish farmers were interested in what Luke shared. As Becca and her aunt served pie and coffee, Luke answered questions and fielded his own. He glanced at Becca as she quietly replenished coffee and provided seconds for some of the men. She seemed so at home in this Amish gathering, which made him realize this was where she belonged. She had questioned remaining in her faith, yet he could envision her nowhere else. If only she realized it as well. Although the idea of Becca staying within her faith was reassuring, it also made him realize how much he would miss her. Even if he returned to his father's cabin, he doubted he would infringe on Becca's life. He imagined her settling back into her routine quickly and finding new meaning in her Amish world. Much as he hated to have her leave him, he knew it was what needed to be done.

After the table was cleared, the men headed to their buggies. Caleb and Luke followed them outside and chatted even longer until the last neighbor had driven out of the drive and turned on to the road home.

"Your words were well received." Caleb patted Luke's back.

He appreciated the older man's praise. "I learned much from them and will incorporate their practices into the workshops I provide in the future."

"You mentioned leaving tomorrow."

Luke nodded. "You have been so gracious and hospitable."

Caleb stopped for a moment and pointed along the

road. "My neighbor told me tonight he is ready to retire and join his children in Ohio. He is a *gut* man, and I will miss his friendship and help. His farm—forty acres of fertile land—will be for sale within a few weeks."

"It is an Amish farm, Caleb, that needs an Amish family."

"I have not known you long, Luke, but we have worked together, and you have shared your views on how to replenish the land. In my opinion, you farm like an Amish man. Some men do leave the ways of the world and embrace the plain life. It is something to consider." He glanced at the house. "Especially if there is an Amish woman who has a place in your heart."

"My heart is not the problem, Caleb. Hers is, but I thank you for letting me know about the farm. I am certain the Lord will provide a *gut* neighbor for you."

Caleb looked at him for a long moment and then nodded. "*Yah*, *Gott* will provide."

Luke followed Caleb into the kitchen. The dishes had been washed and returned to the cupboard and the additional tables and chairs returned to the storage area.

Caleb headed upstairs and left Luke to himself. He settled into a rocking chair by the woodstove and picked up the Lehman family Bible that sat on a nearby table. The Scripture was in German. Luke had studied the language in college, and although he was rusty on grammar and verb agreement, he tried to understand the text that he had opened to, Jeremiah 29:11. He struggled to make meaning of the German and settled on his own paraphrase of the Scripture.

"For I know the thoughts that I think toward you, saith the Lord, thoughts of peace, and not of evil, to give you an expected end."

EIGHTEEN

Becca woke with a start. The house was quiet, but she had dreamed of leaving Luke and had cried out in her sleep. She hoped no one else had heard her.

Today, they would meet the journalist, so she folded her Amish dress and apron and carefully tucked them, along with her *kapp*, into her tote before slipping into her jeans and a clean blouse and sweater.

Remembering back to the first day on the road with Luke, she had enjoyed wearing fancy clothes and had been eager about her new adventure. The adventure had led to her Amish relatives and the realization that she would not find the peace she longed for outside the Amish community.

She stripped the sheets and pillowcase off the bed and tied them into a neat ball and placed them on the side chair. After fluffing the pillow, she covered the bed with the pretty quilt her aunt had made as a girl. Some of the patches were from dresses Aunt Lizzie and Becca's mother had worn as children. Both women had pointed them out numerous times as they recounted stories of their youth.

Becca ran her hand over the fabric and thought of her mother and how much she missed her. She would miss Aunt Lizzie and Uncle Caleb, too. Saying goodbye was always hard for Becca, and today's goodbyes would be especially painful, although nothing would compare with saying goodbye to Luke.

She shook her head, refusing to think about that parting and focused instead on what Rex would reveal about Luke's father. If only he could provide the final pieces of information about the project Luke's father had developed. It seemed the Institute had been involved in stealing the project and claiming it was their own, which was why Luke's dad had left and moved to Mountainside. But where had he hidden his papers and the data needed to reproduce his work and then market it for distribution? Increased crop production would be a boon to the world, especially when so many factions were trying to limit farm production and switch to synthetically produced foods, which she had heard Luke mention when he talked to the farmers last night.

Becca pulled back the curtain and stared into the darkness, seeing the stretch of land where crops were grown and livestock grazed. Why would anyone want to change the blessings of God's creation and the bounty of the land that provided for the needs of so many?

She was only an Amish woman who wanted to go back to her roots and continue the life her mother had lived. Her mother had been so content even though Becca's father had been a difficult man at times.

Becca had never found love within the Amish community, but now that she had gotten to know Luke, she knew how special love could be. Her growing feelings for the *Englischer* helped her realize how attraction for a *gut* man could change a woman's outlook and make sacrifice and hard work worthwhile. Luke had helped her learn so much about who she was and what she wanted in life. Right now, she wanted to fully embrace the faith her mother had taught her as a young child.

Footsteps sounded in the kitchen below. Knowing Aunt Lizzie was probably brewing coffee and beginning her day by making breakfast, Becca grabbed her tote and headed downstairs.

Lizzie turned when she entered and smiled. "You are leaving today, *yah*?"

Becca nodded. "To meet the journalist, then Luke will drive me back to Mountainside."

"As I told you, Becca, you are welcome to stay here."

"*Danki*. Living with you and Uncle Caleb is what I want as well, if you are sure about your offer."

"We are more than sure." Lizzie smiled. "This is what we want, but what about Luke?"

Becca was taken aback by her aunt's comment. "What do you mean?"

"I mean, would he consider coming here? Caleb told him last night about Abe Troyer's farm being for sale. It adjoins our own property and has fertile soil and excellent pasture. He is selling his livestock along with the farm."

"But Luke is returning to Kentucky."

Her aunt's brow raised. "Perhaps he needs encouragement to make such an important change in his life."

"He has his work and his future."

"And he could have both here as well."

Becca placed her tote by the door, not wanting to continue the subject when she had no way of changing Luke's heart. She wrapped her arms around her waist and turned back to her aunt. "Memories of my mother are so powerful here in your home."

Lizzie nodded with understanding as she cut the cold butter into the flour for the morning biscuits. "Your mother loved visiting. Before she and your father met, she stayed with us for a few months as she sorted out her own life."

Becca removed mugs from the cupboard. "My mother was confused about the direction of her life?"

"She was confused about accepting the Amish faith. Your mother was a dreamer in her youth. She wanted to see the world, and the world looked glamorous and exciting."

"How did coming here help her?"

"She worked at a restaurant in town and met a young man. An *Englischer.*"

Becca leaned against the counter and focused on Lizzie. "She fell in love?"

"*Yah*, and she had to decide whether to leave the Amish life or leave the young man."

"And she chose her faith?"

"The young man—his name was Robert—had a job offer in Texas. He wanted her to go with him."

"How did he feel about being Amish?"

Lizzie shook her head. "He had no desire for the plain life. He could see no purpose in living without electricity and motor vehicles."

"And my mother realized she did not want the fancy world and returned home."

"*Yah*, it is so. She returned home, was baptized and eventually met your father. You remember him as a difficult man, but he was not so in his youth. He loved your mother and wanted her to be happy, although I think she always had a spot in her heart for Robert."

"Such hard decisions. I had no idea my mother struggled with the faith."

Lizzie rubbed her hand over Becca's shoulder. "You are not the first Amish woman who has questioned the direction of her future."

"But will I always carry the memory of Luke in my heart?"

"Luke is different. Caleb and I discussed this last night when you were on the porch. There is much in Luke that is drawn to the plain life. If anyone could make the change, I believe he could."

"But he does not realize what he could have living Amish."

"He cares for you, Becca, and I see the way you feel about him. Have you told him?"

She shook her head. "I wanted to say something last night, but after the reporter called, he talked about going back to Kentucky. His mind is set, and anything I say would not make a difference."

"*Englischer* women sometimes speak their mind. Think about that, Becca. Be forthright with your feelings or you might regret not doing so."

Becca thought for a moment. "Are you saying that my mother should have told Robert about the way she felt?"

"Your mother did tell him, and he made the decision to leave anyway, but it helped her to know that he was not the man for her. As I said, she returned home, met your father and eventually they fell in love."

"And it would have been harder for her if she had not shared her feelings?"

"She would have always wondered what would have happened if she had told Robert. Because she did share her feelings, she knew her decision was the right one."

Becca didn't know what to think, and she didn't want to expose her true feelings to Luke and then have them rejected. Remaining silent was a safer option.

Footsteps sounded in the hallway. Luke entered the kitchen. He, too, had changed back into *Englisch* clothing and was wearing jeans and a shirt. He gazed at Becca, and she felt an arrow pierce her heart.

"Morning, Luke." Lizzie pointed to the stove. "The coffee is ready. Breakfast won't be long."

"I wanted to help Caleb with the chores before I left."

"That is very considerate of you."

"I enjoyed my time with him. It is the least I can do." He placed his bag next to Becca's, grabbed his hat off the wall peg and hurried to the barn.

Watching him from the window, a lump formed in Becca's throat. Her eyes burned as she blinked back tears and washed the dishes Lizzie had used to make the biscuits so her aunt would not see her sadness.

Here in this idyllic Amish community with her aunt and uncle, Becca had found what she wanted for her future. Getting over Luke would take time. Just as her aunt had implied, Luke would always have a place in Becca's heart.

Saying goodbye to Becca's aunt and uncle had been hard, and leaving the beautiful countryside and expansive farm saddened Luke. Feeling connected to the Lord, thanks to Becca's example, he internally uttered a short prayer.

Lord, keep Becca safe and let her find her own true love and future happiness. More than anything, I want her to be happy.

"You're quiet," he finally said when they had ridden a few miles in silence.

"I'm thinking of what Rex will reveal and whether we'll run into the security guard again."

"At least I was able to find the tracking device, but that doesn't mean we won't remain vigilant." He glanced at his phone perched on the console. "Once Rex calls, we'll know what direction we should head."

He didn't mention their kiss last night that the journalist's call had interrupted. Luke had been wrong to have been so forthright and recognized Becca's surprise when she stepped out of his arms. As much as he had wanted to kiss her again, he knew that never would happen.

They both seemed deep in their own thoughts as the miles sped by. Luke frequently flicked his gaze to his rearview mirror and the side mirrors to make certain they weren't being followed. There was no sign of the white SUV or the black sedan that the bald man had driven, which was a relief.

Ten miles from town, Luke's cell rang. He pushed Accept and raised the phone to his ear.

"I'm waiting for you at a roadside diner east of town." Rex provided the name of the place and the address. "It's near the old county park."

Luke knew the spot. Miss Hattie had taken him there with Nate to picnic and enjoy the fresh air and playground.

"It sits next to a gas station and convenience store," Rex added.

"We should be there in twenty minutes." He disconnected. "Rex is waiting for us."

Becca nodded. "I hope he provides the information you need."

"I hope so, too."

Just as he had calculated, twenty minutes later he pulled into the parking lot, then, feeling exposed in front of the small eatery, he drove to the rear of the diner and parked there.

Becca's face was drawn as he hurried her inside through a rear entrance.

At this time of the morning, the place was deserted except for a twentysomething guy behind the counter. "What can I get you folks?"

"Two coffees."

Once they had their cups of coffee, Luke motioned Becca to a booth in the rear and sat facing the main entrance.

"What if Rex doesn't show?"

Luke shook his head. "I'm not sure what we'll do, but let's give him a few more minutes."

He drummed his fingers on the table and kept his gaze fixed on the door. A wall clock ticked off the minutes, and his pulse picked up a notch when a man entered the diner. He was dressed in jeans and a tweed sports jacket and wore dark-framed glasses. He greeted the guy behind the counter and then headed to where Becca and Luke sat and shook their hands.

"I read your article in *Farming Life*," Luke shared after Rex had slipped into the seat across from them. "What type of project was my father involved in?"

"A new product, all natural, that would enhance not only seed but also crop production. Andrew Thomas was an altruistic man who was concerned about the growth of large industrial farms and the practices they used, including harmful pesticides and techniques to increase production, but to the detriment of the consumer. Also, I'm not sure if you've been following the trend to push plant-based meat on the world. It's a global initiative, but it's taking hold in the United States, and the big, mega meat-production plants are hopping onboard. The cost of feed is up, transporting livestock to the slaughterhouses and then on to the market is sky-high, and with increased inflation, those prices won't come down in the foreseeable future. Everything in agriculture is the bottom line and how much money the big farms can make. Your father was ahead of his time, and his project would have benefited the world. He was negotiating with a Christian-based supplier to distribute his product worldwide at minimum cost, starting in countries facing dire food shortages. People in Third World countries are starving. Your father's research could have changed that."

"What happened?"

"The Institute said the project belonged to them and that your father was merely one of a number of scientists working on the initiative. They claimed he stole the data and planned to market it himself."

"That's when he left the Institute."

"Exactly. We kept in touch, but only through his lawyer."

"McWhorter?"

"That's the one. As far as I know he was the only person who knew where your father was holed up."

"I tried to contact him."

"And you were unsuccessful because the lawyer was killed in a home invasion about a week ago. The police said it was a gang of kids who ransacked his home and took his high-end electronics."

"Are you saying whoever killed him wanted the computer to learn more about my father's location?"

"I wouldn't have thought the lawyer would have kept the information on his computer, but hackers are good at gaining information, maybe from a deleted file or something rather obscure. Perhaps he had a letter from your dad with a postmark and your dad's address."

Becca touched Luke's arm. He turned to see her troubled gaze. "If they determined where your father lived, they could have learned about his weekly stop at the bakery."

Rex nodded. "The Institute has worked on pyrogenics in the past. My hunch is they set that explosion to get rid of Andy. Without him in the picture, they could market his product—only they soon learned there was a problem."

Rex glanced around before he continued. "Andy told me he gave part of his data to his assistant."

"Joe Morris," Becca provided.

Rex nodded. "That's the guy, only he was in an accident and ended up with a lot of medical problems."

"And the other half of the data?"

"Your father kept that. He didn't want the Institute privy to his project, so he altered some of the data he left behind. They thought they had it all, but I did a little checking since we talked. Rumor has it that the day after Andy's death, the chief scientist realized they'd been scammed. Turns out they had killed the only man who could help them. Unless—" Rex held up his finger. "Unless they could find where Andy kept his records."

Luke pointed to Becca and to himself. "That's why they are coming after us. Do you know anything about where the data could be hidden?"

"No clue but let me know if you uncover anything. Your father and I had planned to meet. I wanted to write a follow-up article and expose the Institute for their evil practices. That article is even more important now."

"I've got the phone number for a security guard at the Institute who was following us until I located a tracking device he had placed on my truck. His first name's Hank." Luke retrieved a slip of paper from his shirt pocket and handed it to Rex. "Here's his number."

"Thanks, Luke. Every bit of information helps."

Becca leaned forward. "A bald man was interested in

the project. He's also been following us, but he does not appear to be involved with the Institute."

Rex rubbed his chin. "There's a philanthropist who wanted to buy the product, although he's not bald. He planned to market it globally and was negotiating deals for a huge profit." Rex pulled up a photo on his phone and held it up for Luke and Becca to see.

"The tall man in the middle of the crowd is the so-called do-gooder. In actuality, he's out for his own profit."

Luke took the phone, stared at the picture. Becca leaned closer.

She pointed to the screen. "Can you increase the size of the photo so we have a clearer view of the people standing behind the philanthropist? Specifically the man in the black jacket."

Rex did as she asked. "I never noticed that he appears bald."

Once again Luke and Becca glanced at the enhanced photo. "That's him," Becca said. "That's the man who attacked me."

"If so," Rex said, "he's working for the philanthropist and probably wants to go around the Institute. No telling what he would do to have that product for his own."

"So the bald man," Becca said, "didn't cause the explosion because he wanted to find Andy. But once the explosion went public, he arrived on the scene and tried to find the hidden data."

"I'll look into him again and let you know what I find out." Rex glanced over his shoulder. "Right now, I need to be going. You folks—"

His phone rang. Rex pulled it to his ear. He listened for a few seconds, then disconnected and pointed to the door. "Get going. Now. Out the back door."

"What?" Becca's heart pounded a warning.

"Go now. I'll warn the kid behind the counter."

Luke grabbed Becca's hand and ran for the door. Rex yelled at the clerk who, thankfully, followed him outside. Before Luke and Becca could crawl into his pickup, an explosion rocked the air. Becca screamed.

Smoke and ash filled the sky. Fire licked at the roof of the diner. A blast of hot air blew past them.

Rex grabbed Luke's arm. "I'll handle the authorities, but you need to get out of here. The guy who called knows someone at the Institute. Don't go through town. Head south and hook up with Rural Route 3. That will take you to the Georgia state line. You've got to get out of Tennessee before they find you. I'm going into hiding. Pray for me. I'll pray for you."

Sirens sounded in the distance as firemen and law enforcement headed to the remote spot. Luke stared at the gray smoke rising from the diner as he helped Becca into his truck. His stomach soured, and fear tangled around his spine. Had they remained, he and Becca would have been killed.

Becca couldn't stop trembling. If Rex hadn't received the warning phone call, all of them would have been in the diner. Her head pounded and her pulse continued to race as the memory of the explosion at the bakery in Mountainside came back full blast—the smell of the burning embers, the hint of gasoline, her attempt to save Andy. Her eyes burned with tears that threatened to cascade down her cheeks.

She shook her head and glanced out the passenger window, but she wasn't seeing the passing countryside as they raced away from the diner. Instead, she was seeing the black cloud of smoke and hearing the explosion that had cut through the diner today as well as the one at the bakery. The memories of both incidents replayed in her mind.

"Why, Luke, why?" She could not understand anyone who would be so evil as to kill Andy and try to kill all of them today. Who knew if others had died because of the Institute's desire to make money?

"I always read that power corrupts," she said. "But I am convinced money corrupts even more."

"I'm grateful Rex was warned."

"I am also thinking of your father. Why did he have to die?"

"So the Institute could control his secret project—only they don't have the correct data, which is making them even more aggressive. Pray that I can get you home before anything else happens."

"The bald man knows where I live, Luke."

"That's why you need to stay at Katie's house, along with your brother. I doubt they would come after you there with Katie's father, her brother and Daniel all on alert."

"What about you? I feel certain the Gingerichs would have room for you as well."

"I'm going back to wherever Rex is staying. I want to work with him. Someone at the Institute is responsible for both of these explosions and—" he glanced at Becca "—my father's murder. It's probably more than one person. The people at the top are most likely involved, and they need to be brought to justice."

"Be careful, Luke. Besides, I thought you were going back to Kentucky."

"I will eventually. I still have the flash drive from my father's assistant. It won't provide enough information, but it will be a start. I know a scientist who is a righteous man. I'd like to show him the files and get his opinion.

He might know someone who's trustworthy and could get a feel for where my father's research was headed. Something that might help another scientist recover my dad's work."

"One thing has changed since we left Mountainside."

He glanced at her. "What's that?"

"You now claim Andy as your father. That is a change for you, and it is what I had hoped for."

"That's because of your encouragement, Becca. If not for you, I would still be in Kentucky not even aware he had died, nor would I know what kind of man he really was."

"Then *gut* has come from all this."

He glanced at her, and the look in his eyes made her take his hand and hold it tight. The thought of his kiss last night returned, and she wanted to be in his arms again. But that was foolish. She knew it. Surely Luke did as well.

Becca continued to check for a white SUV and black sedan as they drove south. Relieved that they weren't followed, she was glad Rex had provided directions that took them on back roads. They passed through a few small towns where children waved from their porches and people nodded as they drove down the main streets. They passed a sheriff's office and saw three deputies talking among themselves on the steps of their headquarters. The town seemed nice and not too far from the Georgia state line.

She started to relax and even felt a bit enthused about seeing Daniel and Katie again. Her brother hadn't returned her call, but he was hesitant to use his phone for anything other than business. Darkness would fall before they got to Mountainside, and she hoped Luke would stay the night.

Maybe she would take Aunt Lizzie's advice and share her feelings with the handsome *Englischer*. At least she would know that he understood the way she felt and how much she wanted to see if they could work something out together. She would share about the Amish way of life in case he would be interested in trying the lifestyle for a period of time.

Lulled by the scenery rolling by her window, Becca rested her head back and closed her eyes. She drifted into a light slumber and was startled awake by the sound of a siren.

Jerking upright, she glanced at Luke, who was peering at the rearview mirror.

"What's wrong?" she demanded.

"No clue. It's a sheriff's car, maybe from that last town we passed through. I'm pulling over."

He edged the truck to the side of the road, rolled down his window and killed the engine. After pulling his driver's license from his wallet, he removed his insurance card and registration from his glove compartment as the officer stepped to the driver's window.

"Keep your hands where I can see them," the sheriff's deputy said.

"Yes, sir." Luke placed his hands on the top of the steering wheel. "I've got my driver's license and insurance card for you."

"Hand them to me slow and easy."

"Was I doing something wrong, Officer?"

The guy in uniform grunted, took the offered identification and glanced over it quickly.

"Open your door and step onto the pavement. No fast moves."

Luke did as the deputy requested.

"Now turn around and place your hands behind you." He slapped on handcuffs.

"Ah, Officer, is this necessary? I'll comply with your orders."

"Easy enough to say." The sheriff peered through the open door at Becca.

"Ma'am, you keep those hands up."

Her heart lurched. "Is there a problem, Officer?"

"Looks like there could be. I'll need to see your identification."

She glanced at Luke then back at the sheriff's deputy. "I do not have a driver's license or other identification."

"That's hard to believe, ma'am."

"I… I'm Amish."

The sheriff took in her clothing. "You don't look Amish."

"Perhaps not, but that's exactly what I am."

A second law enforcement vehicle pulled to a stop behind the first one. The officer approached the truck.

"Check out the passenger. She says she's Amish."

The second officer, sporting a shock of red hair, opened the passenger door and motioned her to the side of the road, where she was handcuffed.

"I have not done anything wrong," she insisted, her heart pounding with frustration and anxiety.

"You're traveling with a criminal."

"Luke is not a criminal."

"He's wanted for stealing information from the Tennessee Research Institute."

Luke started to turn around. "I've done no such thing."

The deputy pushed Luke against the car. "You also caused injury to an infirm man at a nursing home and planted an explosive device at a diner near Waterbend."

"I did none of that."

The sheriff quoted Luke's right to remain silent, but all Becca could hear was the static from the sheriff's deputy's radio and the words he had said about Luke being a criminal.

"We'll take you in to headquarters," the second deputy told Becca. "You'll be able to call a lawyer."

"A lawyer?"

Luke grimaced as they shoved him into the back of the first squad car. Becca was herded into the second vehicle. She was worried about Luke more than about her own situation. Why did they think he was a criminal? It was the Institute who had found a way to stop Luke, just as they had stopped his father.

She hung her head and prayed silently. *Gott help us. Save us. Save both of us.*

Gott must have heard her prayer, because she was released after being questioned. Someone had retrieved her tote from Luke's truck, which was impounded. She had tried to see Luke, but the deputies refused her request and said her best option was to take the afternoon bus that would head to Georgia and eventually to Mountainside. Boarding the bus without Luke was heartbreaking, but she couldn't stay in the small rural town without money or a room.

Luke wasn't a criminal, but the Institute was after him. The sheriff had allowed her to make a phone call. Instead of calling her brother or a lawyer, she had retrieved Rex's number, which she had thankfully copied and tucked into her tote.

The reporter promised to see what he could do, although she didn't know if he had enough clout to help Luke.

The bus rolled into the station, and she found a seat

in the rear, settled against the widow and peered at the jail, wishing she could catch sight of Luke.

If she could have talked to him, she would have told him how she felt, although now it was too late. She dug in the bottom of her tote and pulled out the Bible Luke's father had given her. Holding the small book in her hand brought comfort. She opened it to a favorite Scripture, then flipped through the pages, homing in on words that she had grown up hearing and had taken to heart. If only Luke could have understood the Scripture as well.

She turned to another page and stopped, seeing a few words that were underlined. Strange that Andy had done so only in this one section of his Bible. She flipped through the Bible before she returned to the marked pages.

Her eyes glanced from one underlined word to another, and her heart hitched. Had Andy provided a message in a type of code? Stringing the underlined words together provided the following message: *Thee will unfurrow the garden where the pearl of great price is kept.*

Pearl of great price? The treasure? She read the underlined words again. Andy wasn't telling her about a pearl. He was telling her about the pearl of great price that he had buried. The information about his project.

She thought back to the day at the bakery, when he had given her his Bible. "It has everything you need to know within its pages," Andy had told her.

The door key to his cabin as well as a small silver key were taped to the back cover. Luke's name and phone number were written in the Bible, and now she had found an underlined coded message. Andy was telling her that he had buried the treasure—the data and the information about his project. He had buried it, but where?

NINETEEN

Becca awoke the next morning grateful that Katie and the Gingerich family had taken her in. Even Daniel had been understanding as she explained what had happened and that Luke was being held by the authorities.

"There is a lawyer in town who might be able to help," her brother suggested. "I will call him when his office opens."

"But he practices in Georgia," she said. "I'm not sure he would be able to do anything in Tennessee."

"A phone call is a start, Becca. We will trust something *gut* will come from it."

Becca rubbed her hands together. "Have you seen the bald man again?"

"The day you left, a black sedan drove by, and I wondered if he could be searching for you or Luke." Daniel glanced at Mr. Gingerich for confirmation. "We have not seen the car since then."

"Katie has some errands to do in town," Mr. Gingerich said to Becca. "Would you like to go with her or stay here and rest while my son and I help Daniel at his farm?"

Becca decided to stay at the house to wash the breakfast dishes and bake bread for the evening meal. To her credit, Katie understood her future sister-in-law's need for a quiet morning to sort out her feelings about what had happened.

"You know in your heart that Luke is not a criminal," Katie said after the men had left for the Klein farm. "But I see something more in your eyes. This Luke is a special person, *yah*?"

Becca nodded. "Yet he is *Englisch* and will remain *Englisch*."

"And you will remain Amish?" Katie stated it as a question.

"I went to Tennessee with Luke to help him learn more about his father, but I also needed to learn where I belonged, whether within the Amish community or in the fancy world."

"And you found your answer?"

"Staying with my aunt and uncle helped me realize what is important in life—faith, family, community."

"And Luke?"

"That is the problem. I found out he is important, too."

"I will pray that he is soon released from jail and that a resolution can be reached."

"*Danki* for your prayers, Katie, but I believe this problem may never be resolved."

After Becca washed and dried the dishes, she kneaded the dough for the bread and placed it on the back of the stove to rise.

Hurrying to the guest room where she had spent the previous night, she picked up Luke's father's Bible, which she had placed on the table near her bed. Once again, she turned to the underlined words and reread them, homing in on "the pearl of great price."

Andy's cabin was not far from the Gingerich farm. If she took the trail through the woods, Becca could get there and back while the dough was rising. She wanted to examine the garden Andy had planted in hopes of determining if he could have buried the information there.

Daniel and Mr. Gingerich had not seen the black sedan for days. The bald man had more than likely returned to where he worked with the philanthropist. She would be careful and cautious and would scan the area around the cabin before venturing close to the garden.

She called for Sadie, knowing the sweet beagle would enjoy the romp. "Let's go, girl. We will take the shortcut and be back before anyone returns to the house."

Sadie stayed at her heels until they neared the cabin, and then she raced to the Adirondack chair where Andy had enjoyed spending his afternoons.

"I know you miss him." Becca patted the dog after she had checked the area and found it free of anyone or anything suspect. Not that she could have accosted someone on the premises, but she would have hurriedly retraced her steps along the path and locked herself in the Gingerich home.

Relieved that they were alone, she motioned for Sadie. "We need to inspect the garden."

The dog followed Becca through the garden gate. Becca grabbed the shovel propped against the fence and dug in various areas of the cultivated soil, uncovering potatoes and beets. She laid them to the side and realized she did not have time to unearth the entire plot of land by herself. Daniel would help her, she felt sure, and decided to return at a later time with her brother.

Carrying the vegetables in her arms, Becca headed toward the path. Once again, Sadie ran to the Adirondack chair and barked.

"Come on, girl." Becca patted her leg to encourage the dog, but Sadie was focused on the large rock that had been artistically arranged among the fall flowers. Becca grabbed the pup's collar and tugged her toward the path. As soon as she let go, Sadie raced back to the boulder and began to dig.

Resigned to let Sadie have her fun, Becca left the vegetables on the porch before she plopped down on the Adirondack chair. Closing her eyes, she allowed the cool breeze to calm her upset. More time passed than she realized, and she opened her eyes to see the large hole Sadie had dug. The dog whined and laid her head on Becca's knees.

Laughing at the beagle's precious gaze, she hopped up. "Are you ready to go now?"

Sadie barked again and ran to the hole she had dug. Becca glanced at the disturbed flower bed and leaned closer. The corner of a metal box was visible in the dirt.

"What did you find?" Becca scooped out more dirt and tugged on the metal box. Her heart rate picked up a notch. The box hadn't been discarded as rubbish. Instead, it had been buried purposefully. Pulling it free from the ground, she smiled, knowing she had found the pearl of great price.

She attempted to open the box, but it was locked. The small key taped to the back of the Bible she had left at Katie's house came to mind. Lifting the box into her arms, she turned toward the path, eager to retrieve the key and determine what the box contained.

A huge presence loomed in front of her. Bald head, black jacket, muddy work boots. "All this time, you knew where the data was kept."

"No!" She started to run. He scrambled after her and threw her to the ground. The box slipped from her grasp.

Sadie growled and tugged at the bald man's heels. He kicked the dog, who yelped but returned to nip at his leg. Once again, the bald man kicked Sadie.

"Run home," Becca commanded, worried about the dog's safety. The pup barked twice, then raced along the path that led to the Gingerich farm. Becca was relieved that Sadie was out of danger, but she worried about her own safety.

She stumbled to her feet and ran toward the woods. He grabbed her and dragged her to the cabin. She tried to jerk free, but his grip was strong. He tied her hands behind her back, threw her onto the porch steps and bound her feet.

"Thanks for providing what I needed," he said after retrieving the lockbox.

"You're working for the philanthropist, but you want the data for yourself, except you can't be sure what's in the box."

He chuckled. "A terrible accident happened on the mountainside today. I can see the headlines—'Cabin burns down. Woman trapped in the flames.'"

"You caused the explosion at the bakery."

He shook his head. "Why would I kill Andrew Thomas, the developer of the largest agricultural breakthrough in years? I needed his information."

"But you were here in town at the time of the blast."

"You're wrong. I drove to Mountainside after the explosion. I had recently learned where Andrew lived, but the Institute folks got here first. They killed him, thinking they had all his data, then quickly realized their mistake. Thomas had altered the information before he left the Institute so the portion they uncovered was invalid, which they realized after the explosion."

"Now you think you have the information, so you're going to burn his cabin and kill me in the fire?"

"I'll open the lockbox first."

"Take me home and I'll give you the key."

"I don't need your help."

He hurried to the tool shed and returned with a pick. "This will break the lock." He raised the pick over his head and slammed it against the box, one, two, three times. The lid remained secure.

He grumbled and tried again, but the box didn't open.

Angered by his failed attempts, he grabbed a gasoline container from his sedan. "The pine straw around the cabin won't take long to catch fire."

"Let me go," Becca pleaded. "I'll give you the key."

"You told me you didn't have any data, but you lied." He pointed to the box on the porch. "Why should I believe you about the key? Besides, I have everything I need now."

He poured the gasoline around the porch, tossed the can aside, then leaned down to light the dried pine needles.

Becca gasped, seeing Hank, the security guard from the Tennessee Research Institute, sneak up behind him.

The bald man jerked upright, realizing he had been followed. "What are you doing here?"

"Getting rid of you." Hank swung a punch and collided with the bald man's jaw. He groaned, then grabbed Hank's shirt, and both men stumbled backward.

From where Becca lay on the steps, she saw the flames lick the edge of the porch. If she didn't get away from the cabin, she'd be trapped in the fire.

Luke had worried about Becca the entire time he was questioned by law enforcement, and although he'd answered truthfully, the sheriff and deputies were reluctant to accept his statements as valid.

After being returned to the jail cell, he had hung his head. "Help me, Lord. I need to find Becca and ensure she's okay. I also need law enforcement to believe in my innocence."

Surprised when the door to his cell opened, Luke looked up to see Rex, the journalist.

"Grab your things. You're getting out of here."

Luke followed Rex outside, where his red pickup was parked. "How'd you do it?"

"I can't divulge names, but suffice it to say I have friends in high places. They made some phone calls and pulled some strings."

"What happens now?"

Rex shoved Luke's backpack into his hands. "My suggestion? Get out of Tennessee. The woman you were with was from Georgia. Might be a good idea to hole up in that part of the country."

Luke didn't need to be convinced. He climbed behind the wheel of his truck and waved goodbye to Rex.

When he crossed the state line, he felt a sense of relief and turned on to the back road that led to Mountainside and the Klein farm. Pulling into the drive, he had hoped to find Becca. Instead he found her brother, Daniel, and his future father- and brother-in-law.

"Becca's at my house," Mr. Gingerich said.

Almost immediately thereafter, Katie turned her buggy into the drive. Her face was drawn with worry. "I got home a few minutes ago, and the house is empty. Where's Becca?"

Sadie barked as she raced into the barnyard. The pup rubbed against Luke's leg, then she took off up the hill.

"What's she doing?" Daniel asked.

The beagle looked back. She barked twice and continued up the hill.

"She's trying to tell me something." Luke jumped in his truck.

Daniel ran to the passenger door. "I'm going with you."

Sadie turned off the road and headed up a narrow path.

"That trail leads to your father's cabin," Daniel said.

Luke's heart lurched. "If Becca's there, she could be in danger."

He accelerated. His tires screeched on the pavement. They raced up the hill, passed the Gingerich farm and headed toward the cabin.

Peering into the distance, Luke's gut tightened when he saw smoke.

"Fire," Daniel shouted.

"Know how to use a cell phone?" Luke pointed to his phone on the console.

Daniel picked up Luke's mobile, tapped in a number and held it to his ear. "There's a fire on the mountain. Appears to be at the cabin of the man who died in the bakery explosion. Notify the fire department and law enforcement." He glanced at Luke. "Send an ambulance as well."

Luke's heart nearly stopped, imagining what could have happened to Becca.

"Dear *Gott*," he cried out. "Protect Becca."

TWENTY

Becca flung herself off the porch. Her shoulders hurt as she landed, but she had to get away from the burning timbers as the two men grappled. Hank had pulled a gun and was fighting the bald guy for control of the weapon.

She stiffened her body and rolled forward, over and over again. Grass and pine straw got in her mouth. She spit it out and kept moving.

A gun fired. She gasped, fearing they would realize she was gone and come looking for her.

A vehicle sounded in the drive. Someone else had arrived who could do her harm. She struggled to keep going. The incline became steeper until the bottom dropped out from under her.

She fell about six feet, landed hard and hit her head. The day turned dark, and she lost consciousness.

Luke saw the bald man holding his chest and stumbling away from the cabin. He grabbed him and threw him to the ground. "Where is she?"

"Tied up in the cabin."

Luke raced into the burning building. Smoke was everywhere. He coughed and covered his mouth with his hand.

"Becca!"

Where was she?

Through the smoke, he saw a figure—not a woman, but a man. Hank, the security guard.

Luke grabbed him. "Where's Becca?"

Hank pulled his gun and fired. The round barely missed Luke's arm. He wrestled the gun from Hank and shoved him out the door.

Once clear of the porch, he handed the gun to Daniel. "Guard both of them."

"But—"

"Amish or not, your sister's life is in danger. Keep the gun aimed on both of them."

Daniel nodded as Luke raced back into the cabin. He climbed the stairs and ran from room to room, checking the closets and under the beds.

Convinced she wasn't upstairs, he hurried back to the main floor, where he checked the master bedroom and the pantry. The smoke was thick, and the roof of the cabin was ablaze.

Sirens sounded, and firemen entered the cabin. Two men grabbed him and dragged him out of the cabin. He didn't want to leave without Becca.

Outside, they administered oxygen, but he shoved the mask aside. "I've got to find her. Becca Klein," he told the fireman. "She was tied up and left inside."

"We'll search for her, but you have to stay clear of the fire."

He fisted his hands, upset to be so useless. Stumbling to his feet, he tried to enter again, but another firefighter stopped him.

"If we have to guard you, we can't find her."

Luke nodded, understanding that he had to let them do their job.

Unable to contain his worry and frustration, he walked

to the edge of the yard where he had stood that first day when Becca had brought him here. He glanced again at the pristine valley, grateful that he had been able to learn more about his father—but only because of Becca. Becca, who was more important to him than his own life.

He glanced over his shoulder, seeing the growing flames and knowing time was running out. Dropping his head into his hands, he prayed again, "*Gott*, please hear me. You have to find Becca."

Tears burned his eyes. He wiped his hands over his face and saw something on the hillside below. Not something, but *someone.* Luke screamed for the EMTs and then slipped and fell the six feet down the incline until he came to rest at her side. Touching her neck, he was relieved to feel a pulse. Quickly he pulled out his pocketknife and cut the ropes that bound her hands and feet.

"Becca, it's Luke. Open your eyes and tell me you're okay."

She failed to respond. The EMTs scurried down the hill. He rubbed his hand over her cheek. "Open your eyes, Becca. Don't leave me."

Fearing the worst, he lowered his face to hers and whispered in her ear. "It's Luke. Answer me."

She moaned, and his heart soared when her eyes fluttered open.

The EMTs treated Becca and suggested she go to the nearest hospital for a complete checkup, but she didn't want to leave Luke.

"I have scrapes and scratches. That is all," she insisted as she crawled off the stretcher. Her blood pressure plummeted and she became light-headed, but Luke was there to support her.

"Take it easy, Becca. You were roughed up pretty badly."

"What about Hank and the bald man?"

"Both are being questioned by the sheriff. I'm sure they'll be spending a long time in jail."

She thought of the lockbox. "Oh, Luke, your father's data."

"You found it?"

"Sadie dug in the flower garden and uncovered a lockbox. Last I saw it was on the porch."

He glanced at the cabin. "Most of the porch is gone."

"The box should be fireproof."

He helped her to the Adirondack chair that was far enough from the house to not be harmed by the fire. After ensuring she was okay, he hurried to search around the porch.

Returning with a charred box, he looked discouraged. "It won't open."

"The key's in the Bible your dad gave me. Take me to the Gingerich home so we can determine what's inside."

He helped her to his truck and into the passenger seat. Daniel sat behind her then Luke climbed behind the wheel. Becca looked back at the burned remains of the cabin.

"Where's Sadie?"

Luke saw the pup digging near the porch. "Looks like she's rooting for a buried bone."

"Get her, Luke. She could get hurt with all the embers until the fire is completely contained."

Luke called for Sadie. The dog came running and jumped in the rear seat of his pickup next to Daniel.

On the way to the Gingerich farm, none of them spoke. Becca seemed too tired, and Luke was still concerned about her well-being.

Once they arrived at the house, Luke helped her inside as Daniel hurried to check on the livestock. "The key for the lockbox is taped to the back cover of the Bible." Becca retrieved the Bible and handed the key to Luke.

He opened the box and peered at a flash drive and a stack of papers. Letting out a sigh of relief, he smiled at Becca. "The papers appear unharmed, although I'm not sure if the flash drive will work."

"Hopefully you've found your father's data."

"Thanks to you, Becca." He glanced at his watch. "I need to get back to Waterbend."

"You're leaving?"

"I want to show the information to Rex. He put himself on the line to get me out of jail. He deserves the scoop on this story."

"You'll come back?"

"I'll need to settle my father's cabin so, yes, I'll come back someday."

"But not to stay?"

He shook his head. "I want to help farmers, Becca."

"You could do that here."

"I don't think so."

A lump lodged in her throat. "Thank you, Luke, for helping me see where I belong."

"You helped me learn about my father. Seems we both helped each other."

He rubbed his hand along her cheek. "Take care of yourself, Becca."

She peered from the kitchen window as he left the house, climbed into his truck and turned out of the drive.

Daniel came inside. "Did you tell Luke how you felt?" He showed more insight than she had expected.

"I had to let him go. He has important work to do—after all, he's his father's son."

"And you, Becca?"

"I'll follow in my mother's footsteps."

Daniel's brow raised. He didn't understand her comment, and she was too worn-out to explain anything to him. Instead, she climbed the stairs to her bedroom. After closing the door behind her, she leaned against the wall and cried.

TWENTY-ONE

"Such a beautiful wedding," a number of people gushed after Daniel and Katie became man and wife. The Gingerich home was overflowing with guests, and buggies lined the pasture. There was a joy in the air, but Becca had a hard time feeling the excitement. Yes, she was happy for her brother and new sister-in-law, but her thoughts were on Luke and what they had shared.

From what Aunt Lizzie had told her, her mother had gotten over Robert, but Becca wondered if the hole in her own heart would ever heal.

Aunt Lizzie and Uncle Caleb had come for the celebration, and Becca planned to go back to Harmony Grove with them. Her suitcases were packed, and her bus ticket was purchased. She would return to Mountainside to visit Daniel and Katie in the not-too-distant future and trusted they would visit Harmony Grove as well.

As Becca headed back to the house, Sadie raced from the barn and stared barking. The sound of a buggy caused Becca to turn as a lone driver pulled into the driveway. She would need to tell the latecomer that the wedding was over, but he was welcome to join the other guests for dinner with the wedding party.

The rig pulled to a stop, and the Amish man jumped down, then rounded the front of the buggy.

He tipped his hat and smiled a rakish grin that curled her toes and made her heart nearly leap out of her chest.

"Luke?"

"I came for the wedding, but I think I'm late."

"You're dressed Amish?"

He pointed to the buggy. "And notice my new mode of transportation."

"I do not understand."

"I'm Amish. Or I plan to be fully Amish after I am baptized. Now I am studying the dialect and the religion. The bishop said it shouldn't be too much longer."

"What bishop?"

"The one in Harmony Grove."

"You're living near Aunt Lizzie and Uncle Caleb? They didn't mention you."

"I asked them not to spoil the surprise."

She nodded. "You are a surprise."

Sadie rubbed against his leg, and he leaned down to pat the sweet pup. "I heard you're moving to Harmony Grove."

Becca nodded. "That is the plan."

"Then we'll be neighbors."

Becca was totally confused.

"Remember your aunt and uncle's friend who moved to Ohio to be with family? I bought his farm."

"But what about your house in Kentucky?"

"I sold it. It's a seller's market, so the timing was right."

"And your father's cabin?"

"I can't part with it. I'm here for a bit of time to fix it up. I thought it would be a nice vacation spot in the winter. Nothing's better than a big fireplace on a cold winter's night."

She sidled closer. "I like fireplaces as well. I do not suppose you have plans to share the cabin with visitors."

"No." He was definite in his reply, which made her heart twitch. Then she thought of Aunt Lizzie and what she had told her about her mother.

"I was thinking of a permanent visitor, Luke—someone to share life with you."

His eyes twinkled. "Why, Becca Klein. Do Amish women reveal their feelings to Amish men?"

She stepped closer and wrapped her arms around his neck. "Only when they know that the person needs to be told the truth. I don't want to be without you, Luke."

"Oh, Becca, I love you so much." He lowered his lips to hers, and they kissed for a very long time.

"How do you feel about marriage?" he added when they came up for air.

"I like weddings. Katie and Daniel's was very special."

"Ours will be as well, if you decide to marry me."

She batted her eyelashes. "Shall I ask you, or did you want to ask me?"

He chuckled. "I've wanted to ask you since that first day I saw you at your door. But to ensure I get the opportunity before you beat me to the punch line—" He leaned closer. "Becca Klein, will you marry me?"

"Nothing would make me happier, Luke. *Yah*, I'll marry you."

They kissed again and again, then turned to see Aunt Lizzie and Uncle Caleb waving from the porch. "It is time to eat."

"We'll be there in a minute," Luke called back to them.

He took Becca's hand. "I wanted you to know that a scientist friend of mine is working on the data we were able to compile from my father's project. He's paired what was in the lockbox with what was on the flash drive from Joe Morris and thinks he has come close to replicating my father's work. If so, we plan to partner with a true philanthropic group that will distribute the product to impoverished countries, just as my father wanted."

"Oh, Luke, that's *wunderbar.*"

"My father will be credited as the main developer, with the new scientist as a consulting source, along with Joseph Morris."

"How is Mr. Morris?"

"He's moving into an assisted living center. Carol Rose is helping him get settled, and evidently they've developed a nice relationship together."

"I'm so glad. And the Institute?"

"The guilty are being brought to justice. Some good people worked there. They claim no tie-in with my father's work and will continue with their own research, although it'll be some time before the Institute can clear its name."

"And the philanthropist the bald man worked for?"

"He claimed the bald guy was working on his own and planned to sell the information to the highest bidder, which may be true."

Becca sighed. "I'm relieved it's over, but what about you, Luke? Will you miss your own work?"

"I'm working with the Amish in Harmony Grove and hope to present workshops in various Amish communities. There is much to do."

Becca leaned her head against his shoulder. "Your father would be so proud of you."

"Just as I'm proud of him." He lowered his gaze before continuing. "There was a letter in the lockbox that my mother had written him some months after we left Waterbend. It seems my father had asked to visit me. She told him I was adjusting to my new life and reconnecting with my father would only upset me unduly."

"As much as your father wanted to see you, he wanted to do what was best for his son." Becca squeezed his hand. "He loved you, Luke."

"*Yah*, I know that now for certain. He put my needs first even though it must have hurt him."

He chucked her chin. "I never would have learned the truth about my father if it hadn't been for you, Becca. He was proud of you, too." Then he lowered his lips to hers and kissed her again before they headed to the house to enjoy Katie and Daniel's celebration, knowing their own wedding would be in the near future.

"Your *datt* brought us together, Luke."

"That's right. My dad and his Bible. Just as he told you, Becca, everything we need can be found within its pages."

"Your father was a wise man and so is his son."

"I'm wise enough to know you're the woman I love more than anything. A woman who will make my life one of joy and faith. We'll have a wonderful life together."

Sadie nuzzled their legs, and they laughed as they patted her, then hurried inside to enjoy the first of two weddings that celebrated life and love, faith and family. Becca and Luke had found the future they both deserved and desired. A future together forever.

* * * * *

Dear Reader,

When an explosion in the Amish bakery where Becca Klein works claims the life of a reclusive older gentleman, Becca notifies his estranged son, Luke Snyder. The *Englischer* horticulturist is hesitant to uncover the truth about his father until two opposing forces attack the pretty Amish baker who all too quickly has stolen his heart.

I pray for my readers each day and would love to hear from you. Email me at debby@debbygiusti.com, write me c/o Love Inspired, 195 Broadway, 24th Floor, New York, NY, 10007, or visit me at www.debbygiusti.com and at www.facebook.com/debby.giusti.9.

As always, I thank God for bringing us together through this story. I hope you enjoyed reading *Amish Blast Investigation* as much as I enjoyed writing it.

Wishing you abundant blessings,
Debby

THREAT DETECTION
Pacific Northwest K-9 Unit • by Sharon Dunn

While gathering samples on Mt. St. Helens, volcanologist Aubrey Smith is targeted and pursued by an assailant. Now Aubrey must trust the last person she ever thought she'd see again—her ex-fiancé, K-9 officer Isaac McDane. But unraveling the truth behind the attacks may be the last thing they do...

HIDDEN AMISH TARGET
Amish Country Justice • by Dana R. Lynn

When Molly Schultz witnesses a shooting, the killer is dead set on silencing her and comes looking for her in her peaceful Amish community. But widower Zeke Bender is determined to keep Molly safe, even if it puts him in the killer's crosshairs...

SAFEGUARDING THE BABY
by Jill Elizabeth Nelson

When Wyoming sheriff Rylan Pierce discovers a wounded woman with an infant in a stalled car, protecting them draws the attention of a deadly enemy. Suffering from amnesia, all the woman knows for certain is that their lives are in danger...and a murderous villain will stop at nothing to find them.

DEFENDING THE WITNESS
by Sharee Stover

As the only eyewitness to her boss's murder, Ayla DuPree is under witness protection. But when her handler is murdered, she flees—forcing US marshal Chance Tavalla and his K-9 to find her. Can Chance keep Ayla alive along enough to bring a vicious gang leader to justice?

DANGEROUS DESERT ABDUCTION
by Kellie VanHorn

Single mother Abigail Fox thinks she's found refuge from the mob when she flees to South Dakota's Badlands...until her son is kidnapped. Now she must rely on park ranger Micah Ellis for protection as they race to uncover the evidence her late husband's killers want—before it's too late.

RANCH SHOWDOWN
by Tina Wheeler

Photographer Sierra Lowery is attacked by her nephew's father, demanding she hand over evidence linking him to a deadly bombing. Given twenty-four hours to comply, she turns to ex-boyfriend Detective Cole Walker, who is sure his ranch will be a haven...only for it to become the most dangerous place imaginable.

Get 3 FREE REWARDS!

We'll send you 2 FREE Books plus a FREE Mystery Gift.

Both the **Love Inspired®** and **Love Inspired® Suspense** series feature compelling novels filled with inspirational romance, faith, forgiveness and hope.

YES! Please send me 2 FREE novels from the Love Inspired or Love Inspired Suspense series and my FREE gift (gift is worth about $10 retail). After receiving them, if I don't wish to receive any more books, I can return the shipping statement marked "cancel." If I don't cancel, I will receive 6 brand-new Love Inspired Larger-Print books or Love Inspired Suspense Larger-Print books every month and be billed just $6.49 each in the U.S. or $6.74 each in Canada. That is a savings of at least 16% off the cover price. It's quite a bargain! Shipping and handling is just 50¢ per book in the U.S. and $1.25 per book in Canada.* I understand that accepting the 2 free books and gift places me under no obligation to buy anything. I can always return a shipment and cancel at any time by calling the number below. The free books and gift are mine to keep no matter what I decide.

Choose one: ☐ **Love Inspired**   ☐ **Love Inspired**   ☐ **Or Try Both!**
                   Larger-Print   **Suspense**   (122/322 & 107/307
                   (122/322 BPA GRPA)   **Larger-Print**   BPA GRRP)
                                          (107/307 BPA GRPA)

_____
Name (please print)

_____
Address   Apt. #

_____
City   State/Province   Zip/Postal Code

Email: Please check this box ☐ if you would like to receive newsletters and promotional emails from Harlequin Enterprises ULC and its affiliates. You can unsubscribe anytime.

Mail to the **Harlequin Reader Service:**
IN U.S.A.: P.O. Box 1341, Buffalo, NY 14240-8531
IN CANADA: P.O. Box 603, Fort Erie, Ontario L2A 5X3

Want to try 2 free books from another series! Call 1-800-873-8635 or visit www.ReaderService.com.

HARLEQUIN
PLUS

Try the best multimedia subscription service for romance readers like you!

Read, Watch and Play.

Experience the easiest way to get the romance content you crave.

Start your **FREE TRIAL** at
<u>www.harlequinplus.com/freetrial</u>.